THE SPLIT-LEVEL GAME

THE SPLIT-LEVEL GAME

LOUIS LORRAINE

CUTTING EDGE

ISBN-13: 978-1-957868-54-7

Published by
Cutting Edge Books
PO Box 8212
Calabasas, CA 91372
www.cuttingedgebooks.com

CHAPTER ONE

THE CHRISTMAS PARTY at Pritchard Electric was off to a fast start. In his glass-enclosed sanctuary, Spencer Hawk sighed, turned from the blueprints covering his desk top, and from the depths of his swivel chair watched the gaiety in the big main office.

He felt a curious reluctance to go out and join the crowd. You see the same faces, hear the same voices, five days a week for fifty weeks out of the fifty-two, he thought—and then you are supposed to get drunk with them once a year. There would be the usual smooching in corners, the swift disappearances of couples into the stockroom, the off-key shrieks of laughter. Spence wondered if it were because he was getting old and soured that the prospect of getting drunk and kissing all the secretaries no longer appealed to him. But thirty-three was not old. Look at the way the Pritchard boys—Cecil and A. E.—were prancing around.

Millie, the switchboard operator, lurched past his door. Her blond hair was several shades lighter than usual, and her red dress fit her about ten pounds ago. The way she was navigating she must have hooked up the night connections some time before. As he watched, she grabbed A. E. and kissed him. A. E. grabbed her right back, kissed her hard, then smacked her bottom and laughed.

Spence grimaced, swinging his chair around to face his desk again. He had some designs to work on, and being kissed by girls could wait.

A woman's thin figure paused outside his office door. "Hey, Spence, busy?"

"Come in, Bertha."

He jumped up and placed a chair for her. She sat down slowly. "Wow. I'm feeling those drinks."

He grinned sympathetically. "I think Ivan Todd mixed the punch."

"No wonder, then. That fool scientist is always experimenting." She smoothed her black crepe over her thin knees, peered sardonically at the gay, cavorting, shouting crowd in the main office. "Eat, drink, and be merry—you idiots."

She sounded bitter. Spence frowned at the drawings on his desk. Might as well roll 'em up and forget them until after Christmas. Not that the company of Bertha Pritchard Foster annoyed him. She was a good sort. Her one bad mistake had been marrying Gilbert Foster, a two-faced, ambitious, smooth-talking type who had wormed his way into the Pritchard Electric Company. And now, as the husband of old Roy Pritchard's daughter, Gilbert was trying to worm his way into equal status with Roy's two step-sons, Cecil and A. E.

"Know why I'm in black, Spence?" she asked.

"Because it looks pretty."

"Because I'm in mourning, that's why." She nodded several times. Spence decided Bertha had taken too many drinks, all right. She was not usually so melancholy.

"Mourning? Why, this is Christmas!" He tried to laugh and shake off his own somber feelings.

"Sure. Merry Christmas. Happy New Year. We're going to blow right up."

"What do you mean? Are you worried about the bomb?"

"Naw. Us—Pritchard Electric."

"Bertha?" came an old man's quavering voice. "What are you doing in here? Come along, you two. Join the folks and enjoy yourselves."

Spence stood up as old Roy Pritchard walked in and put a shaking hand on his daughter's shoulder. She patted his fingers.

"Sure, Dad. I'll be right out."

"You too, Spence. You'll miss all the fun."

"I'll be out soon."

"Leila's coming, isn't she?"

"She'll be here."

He watched Bertha help her father into the corridor. The old man was failing. He had started shaking like that six months ago. He was seventy-eight, and both Cecil and A. E. had been trying for fifteen years to make him retire. Apparently they would soon succeed, unless the old man died first.

Leila. Thinking of her, Spence's mouth turned down. She would soon be here, and with bells on. His wife never missed an office party. In fact, she never missed a party, period. She was the original party girl. When he thought of Leila, he became as depressed as Bertha had sounded a few minutes ago.

Bertha's big mistake had been marrying Gilbert Foster. Spence's big mistake had been marrying his beautiful blond secretary, Leila Davis. Talk about a man making a fool of himself over a woman—Spence clenched his fists so tight his fingers hurt. A fool was what he had been—a blind, stupid fool, falling for a pretty face, blond hair, a sexy figure. How long would he have to keep paying for his impulsive stupidity, for mistaking her sexual allure for finer, more lasting qualities?

"Are you thinking deep thoughts, or may we intrude?" said a suave voice.

Spence got up again. He might as well join the party, he figured. He would get no work done today. "Hello, Ivan," he said. He turned and saw a girl who made every other girl in the office look overblown and gross.

Her chestnut-brown hair, smoothed back from her face, was arranged in a sleek French roll in back. Long winged eyebrows gave a look of questioning to the wide brown eyes. Her mouth, almost too big for beauty, was wide and bow-shaped. Her chin had a deep cleft, and there was a dimple in her cheek. She wore a dark green designer dress, unmarred by flashy jewelry; hers was sophisticated good taste, yet there was something disarmingly simple and child-like about her—in the openness of her face, the candor of her direct gaze.

"This is Kate," said Ivan Todd. "Kate Willoughby—Spence Hawk. She, my friend, is intelligent."

"What a damning thing to say about a girl," said Kate, smiling. She was still staring at Spence and her eyes were grave.

"Hello, Kate," said Spence. He wished he could think of something smart and flippant to say. But he never could think of anything like that until hours too late.

"He's my boss," said Ivan, a quirk at the corner of his thin mouth. "So be nice to him."

"Are you his boss?" Kate asked appealingly. "I never know when he's kidding."

"Not exactly," said Spence. "I'm manager of the new products division. Ivan is head of research. We work together."

"He's boss," said Ivan. Then he added, in a stage whisper, "Except when A. E. blunders in."

Spence did not comment. He did not care to discuss the vagaries of office politics with outsiders.

Someone called to Ivan and he sauntered out, leaving Kate.

"I'm probably bothering you. I'll go," she said, after an awkward pause.

"Not at all. Have a chair. It's pretty noisy out there." She sat down. He offered her a cigarette, and lit it for her. He liked the brightness of her brown eyes, the clean freshness of her skin. She wore little makeup, and her hair was the same color all through, not darker at the roots. He snapped the lighter shut. He was being disloyal to Leila.

"What do you do?" he asked, for something to say.

"I work at the Air Force field—government procurement. Just a secretary," she added with a smile.

"Big place out there."

"Mammoth. Someone gets lost every day. It's easy to get lost out there." She stared down at her cigarette, as if reminded of something unpleasant.

"That's one good thing about a small company," said Spence absently. "You don't get lost in the shuffle."

"Have you worked here a long time?"

"Close to eleven years. Since college. Roy Pritchard took me on green as they come and trained me, groomed me right up the line. He made me an officer three years ago."

And by way of celebration Spence had proposed to his gorgeous blond secretary and they had married a week later. He puffed hard at the cigarette, then tamped it out.

"Ivan says Roy Pritchard is good to work for."

"The best." He wondered how involved she was with Ivan. The scientist was a cool bachelor of forty, as wary as they came. Kate could get hurt. But what did that matter to him, Spence?

"Ivan isn't jealous of you."

He started. "Why do you say that?"

"Oh." She smiled in embarrassment. "I'm sorry. I always seem to burst out with what I think."

"Go ahead."

"I thought you might wonder because Ivan said you were his boss. He's very scientific, you know. He even analyzes himself. He says he wouldn't make a good boss."

"He's head of research."

"I know. But he's actually on his own. Doesn't direct the projects. He says you do that."

Spence smiled. "He underestimates himself." Actually Ivan was right, for he was not good at direction. He became too absorbed in his own work.

"I'm talking too much," Kate apologized. "I'm sorry. And it isn't my concern."

"Maybe you like to analyze, too," he said, so she would go on talking. He was becoming increasingly reluctant to join the party outside the door. He heard a high shriek of laughter, a lusty smack as someone was kissed, and wondered if Leila had arrived.

"Yes, I guess so," said Kate. "People are puzzling, aren't they? The more complex the world becomes, the more complex people become. They seemed so simple when I was a child in Alaska."

"Alaska!"

"Yes. We lived there till I was twelve. Then my parents were divorced and my mother brought me to Ohio, to her home. She hated Alaska."

"Alaska," he said again. "Gosh, I used to dream about going up there to live. It's supposed to be so big and clean. Did you like it?"

"I loved it. I cried and cried when we left."

"Spence!" a woman called. "Hey—Spence! I haven't kissed you yet!"

There was a roar of laughter.

"The party," he said wearily. "Did Ivan warn you?"

She smiled. "He said he would take me home when the kissing started."

"You had better start running, then," he advised. He stared at her mouth. It was sensitive and generous. It looked warm and sweet, and honest and loyal. Not like Leila's mouth, he thought.

"Hey—Kate? Oh, here you are." Ivan strolled in. "I thought I had misplaced you somewhere."

"Someone will steal your girl if you keep misplacing her," Spence warned, getting up as Kate rose.

He went out with them. It was about time he made an appearance. It was odd that Leila had not yet arrived. She was usually right on time for fun.

"Seen my wife?" he asked one of the more sober secretaries.

"Leila? Gosh, she was around here an hour ago or so. I don't know where she went."

An hour ago. Spence set his lips grimly, and went in search of the woman. He walked along the corridor past personnel and the mailroom, back to the executive offices. If she were playing around with A. E. after all her promises, he would give her a spanking plus a lecture. She was certainly old enough to know better.

A. E.'s office was dark and quiet. Spence glanced at the glass-paneled door, then walked on slowly to Roy's office. No one there. Spence started back. As he was passing A. E.'s door again, a movement caught his eye—a flash of red.

He flung open the door. Leila was stretched out on the couch in the dim room, her blond head on the cushions, her long legs curled past A. E.'s body. A. E.'s balding dome was pressed against her breasts, his arms greedily gripping her buttocks.

"Leila!" Spence roared. A. E. fell off the couch. Leila sat up slowly, patting her shoulder-length blond hair until it was neat again.

"Spence, darling, where have you been? We looked everywhere for you."

"I was in my office, oddly enough. Not under A. E.'s couch."

Her laughter rippled. The two men eyed each other with frozen anger. A. E. was not quite arrogant enough to force Spence to an open fight. And Spence liked old Roy too much to bring on a battle with one of the man's step-sons even under this provocation.

Leila stood up, slipped her slender feet into red pumps. "Come on darling," she cooed to Spence, tucking her hand under his arm. "Let's join the party."

"Let's," he said grimly. They walked out together. His legs felt like lead; his heart held no more Christmas cheer than a wooden puppet's.

When they got back to the main office, he looked around for Kate, but she and Ivan were gone. He was vaguely surprised that he felt disappointed.

One of the secretaries lurched toward him. "I haven't kissed you yet, Spence!" she shrieked.

"Why, darling," Leila mocked, her thin eyebrows raised. "Do all the secretaries kiss you?"

"Just as you did," he replied harshly, under his breath.

She was laughing. She probably had not heard. He felt sick and disheartened. A married man, with a beautiful wife. An official of the company. He ought to be happy. Happy New Year.

"Merry Christmas!" screamed the plump telephone girl.

Spence nodded solemnly, poured a glass of Scotch and drank it down straight.

CHAPTER TWO

THE WEEK between Christmas and New Year's is an odd period, a bridge of time suspended in space. People don't want to work, for the holiday spell is on them, and they feel dizzy, happy, and expectant of miracles that will lift them from day-by-day drudgery and the tedium of office routine.

Spence strolled along the sidewalk, glancing idly into shop windows. The stores were doing a rush business, he noted, although the gift season was over. Christmas had been ushered in by a six-inch snowfall. Now the dirty gray slush lining the pavement was all that was left of the gloriously white Christmas morning.

Spence thought about Alaska, the endless acres of fresh, clean, sparkling snow. Clean, he thought. Alaska. How wonderful it would be to get away from the rotten crowd in the suburbs where they lived, the Upper Dales set. To be clean, to start over, maybe start a business of his own. To be rid of Leila.

He stopped and stared unseeingly at a window showing a display of tools. Leila had gone to New York for a week with one of the Upper Dales women, Amy Thornton. Spence had not thought too much about it, until he had discovered that A.E. Pritchard would be out of town on business until after the first of January.

Leila had always been sweet on A. E., even before Spence had married her. Maybe she would not have married Spence if A. E.'s wife had divorced him, as she so often threatened to do. Leila and A. E. might be together in New York. Leila was crazy about

New York—dazzled by the stores, the nightclubs, the endless gay parties.

Yes, thought her husband grimly, Leila was quite a party gal. And he had thought she would settle down, have children, make a home for him. That, surely, was the cream of the jest, and he laughed aloud at himself. A man glanced at him curiously, walked hurriedly past.

Spence started meandering again, strolling aimlessly anywhere. He had not wanted to go home after work. Home was cold and dark without Leila, yet when she was there, they fought. And when she was gone, the house was so lonesome he could not bear it. Being alone too much was horrible. Spence had no one who really cared about him. His father and mother had died years before. Old Roy Pritchard and Bertha were as close a family as he had now. And Roy was getting old, losing his grip. Too bad, Spence thought, that Roy did not have sons of his own. Cecil and A. E. were the offspring of a woman who after a divorce had parted them from their father, had married Roy. His first wife, Bertha's mother, had died two years before. Now the second wife had died also, leaving Roy without a companion—and leaving her holdings in Pritchard Electric to the two boys. For her sake, Roy had given his step-sons considerable authority in company affairs. Now, because he was old, they believed they should, and could, seize all authority...

Spence's thoughts about Roy Pritchard abruptly terminated. Just ahead, Spence had noticed a girl.

She had stopped and was gazing at a shop-window display of winter-sports equipment—skis, parkas, ice skates, heavy coats, caps and gloves. She looked vaguely familiar, with that sleek chestnut-brown hair smoothed back from her clear pretty face, with those long eyebrows curved above wide eyes.

He paused beside her. "Hello, Miss Alaska."

Kate Willoughby spun around, stared at him. "Oh—hello! What a nice surprise."

She was glad to see him. His spirits rose. He nodded at the window. "Thinking of going skiing?"

"I wish I could. No, I'm just dreaming."

"I was just wishing I could take off to Alaska."

She sighed. "Oh—lovely. I wish I could, too."

"Have you had dinner?" he asked on impulse. "My wife is out of town and I hate to eat alone. Won't you join me?"

She hesitated so long he became embarrassed.

"Maybe you have other plans," he suggested, to give her an out.

"No. I was only wondering if you would care to try my favorite spot, two blocks from here."

"I'd love it," he said promptly, so relieved he could have whistled with glee.

"It's a smorgasbord place. All kinds of crazy food," she warned.

"If you like it, I will."

She smiled, her wide, generous mouth opening slightly. "Let's go, then." She tucked her arm through his in friendly fashion as they started walking in the direction of the restaurant. "I get lonesome, too," she confided. "I room alone. And it seems that whenever I get to know someone at the job, he or she gets transferred. My rotten luck."

"It happens." He watched their breaths vaporize as they spoke. The weather was turning colder. Probably the thermometer would hit zero tonight.

At the street corner a sudden gust of freezing wind whipped at them, flapping their coats.

"Oh," she said, shivering. "Feel that wind. Like Alaska."

"I should have hitched up my dog team." They crossed the street, holding on to each other, heads bent against the chilling blast. When they reached the shelter of the corner building, they paused for breath in a doorway.

"Whew—cold!" she gasped.

"Maybe we ought to dream about Florida, instead. This is no time for Alaska," he yelled against the howling wind.

She laughed up at him. In that moment, he wanted to push her back into the doorway, hold her against his body for warmth, and kiss her till they were both breathless.

What was the matter with him? Just because Leila had gone was no reason for him to need a woman.

But Kate was different. She was so clean, so strong, so honest and wholesome. Not like that rotten Upper Dales set and their wild sex games. He frowned. Leila was so crazy about playing those games. She could play them every night in the week if the crowd got together that often.

"Here we are," Kate announced. They turned into a narrow doorway, plunged down several steps to the steaming warmth of a restaurant.

Spence sniffed the spicy, meaty odors with delight. "I hadn't realized I was so hungry."

"Doesn't it smell good? Here's a table."

They took off their coats and hats, then headed for the huge center table with its piled rows of delicious foods. There were salads, hot and cold meat dishes, fish of every kind and variety, vegetables, pickles, olives, candied kumquats, pickled watermelon rind.

He was never sure afterwards just what he had eaten. He was watching Kate, listening to her, talking, laughing, enjoying himself freely as he had not been able to do for three years.

They were both startled when finally they left the restaurant and found a blizzard raging. The streets were covered with a thick layer of snow being packed down to sheets of ice by the creeping traffic.

"Oh—no!" moaned Kate.

"How far do you live?"

"Only six blocks. What about you? Where's your car?"

He shrugged. "At the garage, a block from the office. Clear across town. But don't worry about me. I'll stay at a hotel tonight. No sense trying to get home, then back again in the morning."

"I guess not." They were huddled in the restaurant doorway. "There's a nice hotel up toward my apartment. You could go there."

"I'll take you home first. The wind is letting up a little. Let's go."

They plunged out into the snow-chilled world, heads bent, plowing through the thick fresh snow on the sidewalk. He was glad to see she was wearing short boots. They would help. His own shoes were soon soaked through. His feet were freezing cold.

They did not try to talk as they bent against the wind. They had all they could do to keep their balance and struggle on while the wind lashed stinging snow pellets into their faces.

She tugged his arm, pulled him into the shelter of a building. "Here's where I live," she said breathlessly. "Oooh—can't get—my breath."

"Quite a—storm," he gasped. The wind was blowing the snow horizontally across the streets. Traffic was at a standstill. He made out a bus stalled a block away. Cars were parked haphazardly where they had been abandoned.

"Come inside and get warm," Kate invited impulsively. "I'll make you some hot coffee."

That sounded good. He dreaded battering through the storm again, even the few blocks to a hotel.

So they rode the self-service elevator up to the fifth floor, got out and walked into the hallway. It was a large, modern apartment building, recently built. She unlocked a door, snapped on the lights. "Come on in."

The apartment was so warm and comfortable after the storm outside that he felt dizzy with relief. He shrugged out of his soaked overcoat.

"I'll lay it over a chair in the kitchen," said Kate, taking it from him. "Your shoes are soaking wet. Kick them off and stand over the register."

He accepted her advice. The heat coming up through the iron grill had never felt so good. He shivered as the cold was driven out of his body.

While she was fixing coffee, Spence called the nearby hotel. "I'm sorry, sir, we're full up," said a desk clerk. His voice sounded harried. "You might try the Grand, on Seventh."

He called that hotel, then several more. Kate had come back in the room. He hung up after the sixth call. "Nothing anywhere near," he said ruefully. "Guess I'd better try to get home, after all."

"Oh, no! You couldn't make it. You saw how the traffic was stalled."

"I could go back to the office. I've got a fairly comfortable couch."

"You can stay here." She was setting cups and coffee pot on the end table near him. She didn't look at him, but her cheeks were flushed.

"That could ruin your reputation," he said smiling. "No, I guess the office is the best bet."

"How do you like your coffee?"

"Black and sweet."

She poured while he watched her hands. They were large hands, with long fingers, yet graceful, feminine. He imagined how they would feel on his back, caressing, urging. What was the matter with him? It was crazy to think about Kate that way. He was married to Leila—no matter what Leila was doing in New York, or with whom.

She turned on the radio. The news was all about the storm. "Traffic is paralyzed throughout the county," the announcer said. "All city and county schools will be closed tomorrow. The following concerns have announced they will not be open. We repeat, employees are not to go to work at..."

They listened in silence as the voice went on and on, then Kate finally snapped it off.

"Sounds like the blizzard last year, remember?" she observed. "Things were tied up for three days. You had better stay here. At least, I have plenty of food on hand."

"I hate to impose—"

"Not at all. Let me see about blankets. That couch opens up, you know."

He helped her open the couch. She found sheets and blankets and a pillow, put fresh towels in the bathroom. She even found a large bathrobe for him. He did not question where it came from, but she said, "The brothers of a friend of mine took over the apartment for a couple weeks when I was on vacation. This was one of the souvenirs they left. I never did get it back to them."

He did not reply. Surely, she did not believe that she had to explain anything to him. Come to think of it, she probably had told the truth. She seemed bluntly honest. If she had had an affair, he told himself, she would have said so.

They drank coffee until he felt warm and sleepy. They talked about many things, his work and hers, and her childhood in Alaska. She had seen her father only twice since her parents had been divorced.

"He doesn't care for the States and living in big cities. He gets restless, and pretty soon he goes back to Alaska again. I haven't seen him since I was graduated from college. He came down for that."

"And your mother?"

"She remarried and she and my stepfather live in California. I have three stepbrothers I haven't met."

This girl, he thought, must be terribly lonely. No family, no close friends.

"You know, Ivan Todd isn't my boy friend," she said unexpectedly.

"He isn't?" Spence's brows raised ever so slightly.

"No." She blushed. "He's a guy I go out with and we talk about plays and music. But he's a wary bachelor, I guess. He doesn't want to get serious about any woman."

"And you? Do you want to get serious about any man?"

Their eyes met. Hers were a clear brown, honest, a little shy. "Oh—I'd like to. But sometimes I think, what's the use of being serious? All the nice men are married."

It was odd to be talking to an attractive woman across a mattress, the sheets and blankets opened invitingly. She was sitting on a straight chair on one side of the bed in the small living room. He sat in the overstuffed chair on the other side.

She jumped up. "It's getting late," she said briskly. "You may have your bath first. I'll do these dishes."

She was a careful housekeeper, he thought, as he carried the coffeepot to the kitchen. Everything was in place in the small, neat cupboards, on the immaculate enameled work-table, the small electric range.

He took his bath, soaking luxuriously until even the memory of the chill was steamed out of his body. Then he dried, put on the robe, went to bed. After he had slipped between the covers, he took off the robe and laid it on the armchair.

He rolled over, becoming comfortable and drowsy. Then he heard the water running in the shower, heard Kate splashing around, humming a song. The longer he listened, the clearer became the mental picture of how she looked right this minute. And the wider awake he grew.

She was tall for a woman, about five feet seven or eight. Her legs were long and graceful, but she was far from being skinny. The flesh of her arms was firm and glowing, her body rounded, the breasts firm and full. He stirred uneasily, trying to forget where he was.

He heard the door open as she came out of the bathroom. Then the light snapped off.

"Kate," he blurted.

"Yes?" She paused in the doorway, a dark shadowy figure.

"Come here for a minute, will you?"

In the silence he heard her breathing.

"Why?" she whispered.

"Well, don't if you don't want to."

Silence again. Then the shadowy figure moved away from the door, moved toward the couch-bed. She stood beside him, wearing a long winter nightgown. Her hair hung below her shoulders in twin braids. She was fragrant with the odor of soap and perfume.

He held open the covers for her. For a heart-stopping moment he was afraid she wouldn't come. Then the shadow stooped. She sat down on the bed, kicked off her slippers, and slid in beside him. His arms closed strongly about her. She turned on her side to face him.

"Why?" she whispered. "Why do you want me?"

"I love you," he heard himself saying, and knew it sounded nonsensical. "I mean—I want you. I need you."

It must have been enough. Her arms went around him. He put his hand under her head, bent over her, his unclothed body pushing to her skin. His mouth searched blindly for hers, found it. He kissed her hungrily, kissed the wide sweet mouth he had thirsted for. Her lips were warm, wet, opening under his.

Tentatively he explored her with his lips and hands. Her face, he delightedly discovered, was as soft and warm and kissable as it had looked. He kissed the smooth cheeks, the tender places below her ears, the long winged eyebrows, then her mouth again. He touched her throat, caressed her shoulders, moved downward, sliding in the bed so that he could reach all of her. He kissed the soft fragrant hollow of her throat, opened the nightgown and kissed below, burying his head between her warm full breasts.

Her hands were touching his ears, his neck, the close-cropped hair, exploring him eagerly as he explored her. He covered a breast in one large palm, squeezed excitedly. It was so big and firm, the flesh so vibrant and silky. He found the nipple and played with it, his thumb pressing it into the breast to tease it to tautness. The nipple rose up hard. He pushed the cloth of the nightdress aside, nuzzled his head against her breast and caught the nipple between his lips.

He bit gently, pulling at it. Her hands went to his naked back, the long fingers caressing. He could feel her growing excitement in the way her hands touched him, lightly at first, then stroking harder, then with the fingers beginning to bite into his thews.

He raised himself, felt for her legs, found the hem of the nightdress and pushed it up. Her legs were long and smooth, the thighs silken-soft.

"Let me take it off," she murmured, when the roll of cloth balled uncomfortably between them. He helped her to sit up and together they pulled the gown over her head. She flung it aside and lay down again, sighing with pleasure and anticipation.

She has known men before, he thought. That made it easier for him. His conscience stopped tugging at him. Then he forgot everything in his blind desire for the body beneath his.

He leaned forward, his hands under her armpits holding her firmly. Her hips moved to avoid him, flinching from him.

"Hold still," he muttered.

She cried out, frightened. "Oh—wait! Wait—"

He bent his head and kissed her mouth, her soft, open lips. He plunged his tongue into her mouth, circled it to touch her tongue. Her back arched. He caressed her breasts, pulling at them. They were swollen, big in his hand, the nipples pointed. He smiled. She was ready, whether she thought so or not.

He pushed forward, holding her firmly so she could not move away. She was gasping. He could feel her parting before his lunge as he cleaved the flesh, high, tight, far, hard.

She was moving, crying out. The tremors began to shiver through her body. He felt them communicate to him, so that he also began to tremble. She clutched him with hurting fingers, and he gloried in the pain. She was soft and moist and yielding. Her wide thighs held him, her long legs curled about him.

Then, wildly and freely, he spent himself in a volcanic burst of passion.

Why had she permitted him to stay and enjoy her?

Was she innocent, or didn't she care? At any rate, he was grateful and kissed her soft body as he lay, now calmed and quieted, beside her.

"Kate," he whispered in wonder.

She sighed and curled up against him, her leg between his knees.

"Spence, you don't have to talk. Don't talk."

They slept little that night. But it did not matter. By morning the snow was so deep nobody would want to go out. Certainly not Spence.

He could not bear the thought of plunging into the cold, lonely world. Not with Kate beside him, ready to let him do whatever he pleased with her.

Why should a man be lonely when he could have such a woman?

CHAPTER THREE

L EILA CAME HOME from New York two days after New Year's. She was happy, bubbling. And Spence thought grimly that Leila did not—could not—get that way from going shopping with another woman.

But Spence realized that he had no right to condemn her. He was full of burning guilt about his interlude with Kate. No regrets, he told himself, but he fully realized that the idyll had been out of order. For one thing, it made going back to Leila all the more difficult. He had had a taste of what it was to live with a different kind of woman, a woman who was loving and giving, gentle yet strong.

This was no way to hold a marriage together, he told himself. And at once he resolved to try harder to make a go of it with Leila. They had had enough in common to get married. And there was no denying that she was a beautiful and exciting woman.

Leila wanted him that first night of her return. Someone or something had aroused her strongly, he could tell.

As soon as they were in bed, she was at him. "Did you miss me, darling?" she cooed, touching him cleverly.

"Sure did," he said, trying to sound convincing. "It was awfully lonesome here."

"I'm sorry, sweet. I shouldn't have left you alone for the holidays. But New York is so marvelous. I'll make it up to you," she added generously. And instantly redoubled her efforts.

He managed to give a good account of himself. It was not difficult. No doubt of her attractiveness. The bedside light revealed her in all her lush beauty—the tousled blond hair, the flushed face, her pouting red mouth, the smooth perfect breasts with crimson tips, the concave belly, the white thighs. He watched her as he brought her to bliss, saw her face contort in an expression of dazed pleasure. Then he saw the slack mouth.

She shuddered, ecstasy shaking her body. He rolled away from her. She was finished with him. He was alone. As usual.

She sighed, stretched, got up and went to the bathroom. She took all precautions. She did not want a child.

But Kate had not been careful. She had been reckless, deliciously indifferent. What if Kate had his child? He rolled over on his stomach, trying to forget Kate. No, Kate was not for him. That had been a brief rapturous interlude, but only an interlude-something to be forgotten.

Leila came back, went quickly to sleep. Spence looked long and soberly at her kitten-face as, curled up, she slumbered peacefully. Then he turned off the bed light and lay staring into the darkness.

Next day at the office Spence ran into problems. He had been aware since before Christmas that something was wrong, that the scent of trouble was in the air. But he had been unable to put his finger on just what was out of gear.

But this Wednesday morning, Cecil Pritchard, oozing charm as usual, came into Spence's office about ten. Spence had once thought old Roy's older stepson was a lot like Roy; but long since Spence had ceased to believe it. Cecil had a basically good mind, a feeling and instinct for people, and fine mechanical ability. But Cecil had used his talents coldly, only to satisfy his drive to acquire money. To Roy, financial success had been incidental—the work was everything. Cecil was not like that.

"Spence, boy, I sure hate to bother you. The old man always says you are the new backbone of Pritchard's, now that he isn't inventing any more."

Spence stiffened automatically. Cecil wanted something.

Spence laid aside the drawings and sheets of figures. "No bother," he said, trying to sound friendly. "And Roy is exaggerating. I'm not really inventing much. That's Ivan's department."

"Sure. The team spirit." Cecil eased himself into the straight-backed chair opposite Spence's desk. "You ought to have some comfortable furniture in here. A couple of comfortable armchairs—"

"I like these." The boys were getting soft. Besides, stiff chairs discouraged people from making long visits. "Something I can do for you, Cecil?"

Cecil's balding head dropped as he avoided Spence's gaze. "We were wondering if you could take a quick business trip for us. A. E. is tied up. I've got two conferences scheduled, and it isn't Gil's field. Meeting in St. Louis, Thursday afternoon and evening."

"You mean tomorrow?"

"Yeah. We have plane reservations and the weather has cleared. We were going to skip it but the St. Louis firm is having open house. They have some new products we want to look at. You could examine them and see if we want to start buying the stuff."

"That's a little out of my line. I've been concentrating on our own new products. I don't pay much attention to finished goods."

"I know, I know. But these papers explain. You could go over to Ted's this afternoon and get a briefing. How about it? Will you go?"

Spence hesitated. There was something fishy here, he was sure, but he could not read the signals. "Okay. What time is the plane?"

"Tomorrow morning, eight-fifty. You might as well go from home. And stay overnight, come back Friday. We made hotel reservations for you."

"All right." He accepted the papers and plane tickets. The tickets were already made out in his name, he saw after Cecil left. He must have been confident that Spence would accept.

Bertha Pritchard Foster dropped in at noon. "Buy me some lunch, Spence," she said.

"Sure, Bertha." He took her out, relieved that she was wearing a purple dress. Those black things always looked so somber on her thin frame.

When they had found a table at a comparatively quiet restaurant and had ordered lunch, she told him seriously, "I lured you here, Spence."

"Gee. My lucky day."

"You do good things to a gal's morale. But wipe that grin off your face. I have a feeling that the meeting tomorrow is the beginning of big trouble."

"The open house? What trouble could that be?"

"Open house? What open house?"

"In St. Louis. Cecil asked me to go."

Bertha stared at him. "Cecil's sending you out of town? When?"

"Tomorrow morning. I'll be back on Friday."

Her mouth set, her chin raised belligerently. As she lifted her head, Spence noticed the gray beginning to streak thickly through the rich black hair. Bertha was well into her thirties, and she had had problems.

"Cecil and A. E. are plotting, and they got you out of the way. That proves it to me. They are out to do something irregular, something they don't want you or me or Dad to find out."

"Are they scheduling a meeting here?"

"Yes, at the Grand Hotel. Just Cecil, A. E. and Gilbert. And I found out that officials from Locke and Ace Electric and Golden Electric are going to be there."

Spence stared. He could not believe it. "Ace? Why, Roy hasn't even spoken to them for ten years, since they undercut us in Pennsylvania."

"Cecil writes letters to them—and doesn't keep the carbons in the office files."

"I can't believe—"

Bertha said, "I feel better, telling you. I can't speak to Dad. He mustn't get excited, the doctor says."

Spence stared at his steak. He had little appetite for the meat, and little for intrigue. He liked everything open and above board. "Tell you what. Wait till I get back from St. Louis. Let me mull it over. The old brain doesn't click very fast sometimes."

"But it clicks honest," Bertha said bitterly. "Not like the gray matter of my dear step-brothers, Cecil and A. E. And my husband, Gilbert—especially Gilbert." She laughed. "I might have known such a slick, handsome guy wouldn't be marrying me for love."

So she was waking up. Spence had often wondered, pityingly, how long it would take.

"Gilbert's been voting my stock," she added, playing with a spoon. "He's crazy for power. He never had any before, and now he's like a kid turned loose in a candy store. Only—price-fixing isn't candy, Spence. Not by a long shot, it isn't."

"We can't be sure they're finagling," he said sharply, hating to hear his own suspicions voiced. "Let's wait a while before coming to conclusions."

"If you insist. But next meeting, I'm voting my own stock. Be sure to let me know, Spence, whenever a stockholders' meeting is scheduled. Gilbert doesn't bother to tell me any more."

"I'll tell you," he promised, remembering the last farce of a meeting. Old Roy had come in late. They had "forgotten" to tell him of the meeting, and he had been furious. Bertha had not come; Gilbert had her proxy, he had said. Spence had had little to say. He owned no stock and was there only to report on new products.

Bertha and her father had effectively balanced Cecil and A. E. Now it looked like the two stepsons were taking over, with Gilbert's support...

Spence flew to St. Louis the next day. The St. Louis people welcomed him with cordial appreciation—and with some surprise, even though Cecil had called to say Spence was coming.

"I don't really know why you bothered," confided one official. "We've got just about the same line, and you weren't interested before. This open house is to attract new prospects, not old ones. Is there something special you want that you think we might have?"

Spence went home in a cold fury on Friday morning and called Bertha from the airport. When she answered the phone, he said, "It's Spence. Can you talk?"

"Sure. Gilbert's gone. What happened?"

"Nothing," he told her angrily. "A big hunk of nothing. Cecil was putting me on ice. What happened here?"

"I don't know. Dad wasn't told. Neither was I. And I couldn't ask questions without being suspected. But I know this—my brothers and Gilbert were gone all day. And they left word with their secretaries that they couldn't be reached."

"Something queer is going on, all right," Spence concluded.

"What can we do, Spence?" She did not sound scared. She sounded determined and angry.

"Keep our eyes open. And please, don't sign any more proxy papers. Does Gilbert really have your proxy?"

"He did. But I tore up the papers after the last stockholders' meeting. He was furious. He's been nice as pie lately, trying to get me to sign more."

"Make sure you don't."

CHAPTER FOUR

THE ST. LOUIS jaunt had put Spence behind in his work. He stuck to his desk till seven, then decided to stay in town overnight and work again on Saturday.

He phoned Leila. She was angry. "You promised to go to Amy Thornton's with me," she stormed.

He sighed. Another one of those parties. "I forgot," he said. "And all this work has piled up—"

"Well, I'm going anyway."

He shrugged and hung up. He was tired. He took out the telephone book and turned to the section on hotels. Then on impulse he flipped the pages to the W's. There she was—Willoughby, Kate.

He dialed the number. He would talk to her only a minute. He wanted to hear her voice.

"Hello?"

"Hello, Kate. This is Spence Hawk."

"Spence! How are you?"

"You sound tired."

"I am. I just got home from work."

"Will you have dinner with me?" He had not intended to ask, but now he could not resist the impulse.

She hesitated. "Oh, I'm tired. I'm afraid I won't be good company—"

"Don't, if you don't want to."

"But I do want to."

"Good. I'll pick you up in front of the building in a half-hour."

"All right."

He put his suitcase in the back of the car. He could find a hotel later. Kate was waiting at the doorway of her apartment building when he pulled up. He started to get out of the car, but she ran across the sidewalk and got in.

"Hello," he said.

"Hello." Her cheeks looked rosy, soft. He leaned over and kissed the nearest one. Her skin was as softly pleasing as it looked.

"I didn't mean to call again," he said.

"I know. I had made up my mind not to see you, even if you did call."

He touched her hand lightly. "Where do you want to go?"

"You say."

"There's a place a few blocks from here. The steaks are good."

"Fine."

As he started the car, he had a feeling she would have said "fine" if he had suggested a hamburger at a drive-in. She liked being with him, even though she was trying to fight it, just as he was.

He explained at the restaurant, "I just returned from a business trip to St. Louis that put me behind in my work. I decided to stay in town overnight and work tomorrow also."

"I see. What work do you do? The kind Ivan does?"

"Not exactly. We're on the same projects, but I do the desk jobs, the statistics and drawings. He does the lab experiments, the research, the tests."

"And you'd like to be doing lab work?"

He looked at her over his glass of Scotch. "You're reading my mind."

"I was looking at your hands. They aren't the hands of a white-collar man."

He glanced down at his right hand, flexed it curiously. It was a big hand, lined and scarred with the years of experimenting. His fingers were getting soft now. He had been out of the lab for many months.

He laughed shortly. "Yeah. I'm crazy. Sometimes I'd give anything to trade places with Ivan."

Her wide lips parted in a smile. He watched her, fascinated, as she spoke. He remembered the soft sweetness of those lips under his. "The penalty of success," she said. "I've seen it happen in government, especially the Air Force boys. Crazy to fly, but they've been promoted to desk jobs directing operations. They're like caged panthers."

The music of the three-piece combo was good, so they danced. He could feel her tiredness as he held her.

"Was it a rough day?" he asked.

"A rough week. I worked overtime three nights."

"I shouldn't have asked you out."

Her head, dark and smooth, moved against his shoulder. "I'm glad you did."

He was silent, then, holding her. He felt her body close to his, and he wanted her, with a direct, urgent need that must have communicated itself to her. Her hand tightened in his. Her thumb rubbed against his fingers.

"Kate," he said huskily. "Turn me down if you wish. But I'm asking for another night with you. This night."

Her answer was so soft he had to bend his head to hear. "I want it, too. All right, Spence."

They drove back to her place. She showed him the entrance to the parking garage under the building. He drove the car down the ramp, into the building, and parked. He took his suitcase from the back of the car. They went up the service elevator to the fifth floor.

She unlocked the door, flicked on a light. He went in, set down the suitcase, closed the door and took her in his arms.

Her head lifted to his. He put his mouth down heavily on hers, held her tight and hard against him. The kiss lasted till they were both breathless. She broke away.

"Hey. I get to breathe, don't I?"

"Every once in a while," he said, reluctantly letting her go.

She laughed, but turned away shyly. It gave him a pang to see her uncertain. She knew that he was married, that this affair could never be serious; he would not blame her if she threw him out.

"Do you want some coffee?" she asked.

He did not, but he said, "Sure."

They had coffee, and sat and talked a while. He liked the way she spoke, liked her blunt way of saying what she thought in all frankness and honesty. He liked the way she cupped her chin on her hand and listened to what he said as though it were important to her. Her dark eyes were large, beautiful under the winged eyebrows.

The more he looked at her, the more he wanted her. She stood up to get the coffee pot. "More?"

He stood also. "No. Kate, I want—"

Her eyes got larger as he drew her close.

"Kate," he whispered.

She put her arms around his neck. He kissed her ardently, pressing his hand into the small of her back.

She broke away again. Her face was flushed, her eyes avoided his. "I'll put the coffee things away," she said.

Was she avoiding him?

"You go on to bed," she said. "I'll be along as soon as I take care of these."

He exhaled a sigh of relief. While she rattled dishes in the kitchen, he took his suitcase to the bedroom. It was warm and comfortable there. He liked the crisp red-and-white drapes, the faint scent of Kate's perfume, the wide, inviting bed.

He undressed and slipped under the covers. Kate came in soon afterward. She hesitated about undressing, pulled off her earrings as she watched him out of the corners of her eyes.

He crossed his arms under his head and frankly watched. She made a face at him, took her nightgown from the closet and went to the bathroom to change.

He grinned.

When she came back, she hung up the dress and laid the underclothes on a chair. He waited. She went over to the dresser, unfastened the smooth roll of her hair, and brushed it out. He watched as the hair gleamed and rippled under the brush, hair that hung below her shoulders.

She brushed her hair quite a while.

"Kate," he said finally. "I'll just muss it again. Come on to bed."

She put down the brush, turned off the lights. When she slipped under the covers, his arms went around her. The remembered sweetness of her body aroused him at once, and he began to kiss and caress her. His hand went to her knees, pulled up the nightgown.

"Spence!"

"What, Kate?"

"Not so fast."

"You shouldn't make me wait so long."

She laughed softly, adjusted her body to his as he came over her. Her arms closed around him.

He wanted her so much he didn't wait to take off her nightgown. He wanted her fast and soon. He began the drive at once. He could feel her readiness. He attacked smoothly, waited, attacked again. She surrendered sweetly to him. Her flesh encased him. Soon he was reaching high and far. And it was good, good and satisfying and full and soft.

He rested against her, luxuriating in the sweetness. He put his head against her full breasts and nuzzled at them, biting them softly. Being on her was like resting on the softest, silkiest pillow imaginable, a pillow that moved and breathed and responded to him. No, he thought, it was like swimming in warm water, resting on a wave that gave and trembled. No, it was more like riding the wind, feeling it move and stretch under him, a warm South wind, perfumed and springlike.

He felt her shift under him, felt her loins tighten. He smiled against her breast, began to move, slowly at first, then faster.

They felt it at the same time, with mighty impact. He heard the blood roaring in his ears as his body galvanized, as at the same moment the soft body under his convulsed. He held her tight, rolling back and forth with her, prolonging the ecstasy.

When it was finished, he relieved her of his weight. Tenderly he drew down the nightgown to cover her warmly, pulled up the blankets, and lay beside her. She was so limp, so still.

"Kate," he whispered. "Are you all right?"

He was not sure she heard till she finally stirred, turned on her side and stretched against him. When he kissed her, he tasted tears.

"Did I hurt you?" he asked, alarmed.

"No, no." She rested her face against his bare chest, curled closer. They went to sleep, holding each other.

In the night he awakened and at first could not tell where he was. He touched the woman next to him. She was not wearing Leila's flimsy nylon gown; it was a heavy cotton. Her hair was not stiff with dye, brittle at the ends; it was long and soft and warm. Her breasts were not girlish and impudently pointed; they were big and soft and plump, the breasts of a woman.

Kate, he remembered, feeling her. Kate Willoughby. He was sleeping with Kate. Miss Alaska, he remembered, smiling.

He wakened her with his lips on the plump breasts, greedily drinking at the soft points. He wakened her with his hands under her gown, exploring the warm and secret places. When she opened her eyes, he was ready to attack, ready to possess.

"Spence," she murmured. He kissed the lips saying his name.

He took her in silence and darkness, under the warm covers, moving blindly to find her. Her breasts were swelling, the nipples hardening to points. He took one sweet bud in his mouth, pulled at it. Still holding it, he moved his hips, searched her, found, pressed. Her thighs were damp, limp. She made no resistance. He was soon home, safe, fast.

Her hands played sleepily on his back, tickled down his spine. He settled on her, lay with her a long time...

They slept late. When he awoke, he opened his eyes to find her head on the pillow a few inches from his. Her brown gaze was upon him soberly.

"Good morning," she said.

Her mouth was close. He kissed it. She responded. One thing led to another.

Kate said, "Weren't you going to work at the office this morning?"

"I'd rather work here," he said, working.

She blushed. He loved the soft red flush in her cheeks, the soft glow of her naked skin as he revealed her under the covers. The nightgown had been tossed out of bed.

"But you have so much to do," she protested weakly.

"Later. Hold me, darling."

"Oooh!"

He lifted her hips, forced them in a round and round motion. She learned rapidly. It was fun to teach her.

About noon, he finally got dressed. She put on a robe and made breakfast for him. But she seemed sober and thoughtful.

When she brought him coffee, he drew her to his lap. "Regrets?"

"Oh, Spence, we know this is wrong."

"You didn't enjoy it?" He held her tighter when she tried to get up.

"Too much, Spence. I don't want to get involved."

"It seems to me we're already involved."

"Maybe. Physically we are. You're very—" She looked at him, her brown eyes direct and candid. "You're very experienced. You know how to make love."

"Thanks," he said. "I'll be happy to demonstrate again soon." He touched her bare knee under the robe. She pushed away his hand and folded the robe sternly.

"No. I mean it. You're married. And—and this is foolish of me, to encourage you. It can lead only to trouble."

The lightheartedness, the contentment with her, drained out of him. "I know," he said. "It was selfish of me. I wanted you. I took."

She touched his cheek with her fingers. "No regrets," she said. "I enjoyed it too. But it has to stop. No more."

"No more at all?"

She closed her eyes, shook her head. Her chestnut-brown hair was braided in a single long plait down her back. He took it and began to unfasten it. She let him. He unfastened the hair and spread it out on her shoulders, and kissed the face framed in the heavy softness. Her mouth was soft, sweet.

"No more?" he whispered.

"Oh, Spence, no more. Please."

He drew her over to the couch and lay down with her. And it was as if he had never touched her before and had hungered for her and desired her without having. For her body entranced him and drew him, and he was eager and impatient and strong. He drove and then held, and silently they knew pleasure keener than pain.

When finally he got up, she lay still. He drew the robe closed and fastened the sash gently. She looked up at him with wistful eyes.

"Next week?" he said.

"No, Spence."

He felt cold when he realized her determination, cold and frantic. He couldn't let her go, he couldn't walk out and forget her.

"I'll call you," he said.

"No, Spence."

He touched her face. It was wet. "Darling."

"Don't call me. Please, Spence. Let it end before we get too badly hurt. Please, Spence."

She sat up, her long legs swinging to the ground. Her feet searched for the slippers he had pulled off. He found one under the coffee table and brought it back to her, and kneeled and put it on her long narrow foot. He kissed the foot, and then her knee.

She put her hands on his head. "Spence. Please go now."

"Let me call you again."

"No. It ends here."

"I could come next Friday."

"No. No, I won't see you."

They stood up. He put his hands on her shoulders. She was almost as tall as he was. And she was strong. In many ways she was stronger than he was.

"I don't want to say goodbye."

She smiled a little. "Don't say it, then. Spence—" She reached up and kissed his mouth lingeringly. "Just go."

He found his suitcase and walked out, and she closed the door after him. He went down to his car and drove off.

It was cold outside, cold and still, the sky gray and heavy with cloud. Looked like more snow coming, he thought. He wished he were able to go back to Kate, and wait out the storm with her. He had not wanted to leave.

And he could not, would not, accept her dismissal. He would see her again—and again—and again.

CHAPTER FIVE

THE FOLLOWING WEEK was a long and empty one for Kate Willoughby. She kept thinking about Spence—about his eyes, his grin, his big, hard hands, his tough body that could be such a wonderful instrument of love.

Why, why did he have to be married? She had been looking for a man like Spence all her life, and when she found him he was married.

Her dad would have liked Spence. They were a lot alike, not talking much, good with their hands, powerful, big, controlled. He had a strong confident masculinity that asked no favors. He took what he wanted of a woman. He did what he pleased.

The work let up at the office, and she had too much time to sit and think. She got angry with herself for being so preoccupied with Spence. She tried to rationalize their relationship.

After all, she had had a couple of affairs before this. She had broken off before they had damaged her. All this meant was that when she had met Spence she had been a woman with unsatisfied hungers. As for Spence, probably he was dissatisfied with his marriage. And the two had met at a dangerously lonely time—Christmas. So the result had been—explosion.

But now she had broken off with Spence. All right, it was finished. No one would get hurt.

The phone rang. Startled, she jumped up so fast to answer that she banged her side against an open file drawer.

"Ouch," she muttered, holding her aching side. "Hello?"

"Is this Purchasing?" snapped a voice.

"Yes, sir." She had forgotten to identify the office. She grimaced.

"Colonel Smith here. I want—"

With a sigh, Kate came back to her responsibilities. Spence would not be calling her at the office. Anyway, she had told him not to call her at all, hadn't she?

At home that evening, she stretched out on the couch, with the radio going.

The music was soothing. She could forget her aching side, the weariness in her feet, her bruised heart. It was well, she considered, that she had not let the affair go on. Spence could be a tough guy to forget. She closed her eyes and with a determined effort of will tried to make herself relax. She could forget. She . . .

As earlier in the day, the ringing telephone interrupted her thoughts. She was off the couch and running toward it in a reflective burst.

"Hello?" she said eagerly.

"Hi, Kate. Ivan Todd here."

She felt disappointment choke her.

"Oh, hello, Ivan!" she said with false gaiety. "How have you been?"

"Fine. Say, I've got two tickets to the ballet Saturday evening. They were sold out, but I got them from a friend who can't make the date. Would you like to go?"

"Oh, I'd love to! I tried to get tickets myself last night and couldn't."

"I figured you would enjoy it. Pick you up at six, then, and we'll have dinner somewhere."

"That sounds lovely. I'll be ready. How's everything at the mines," she tried to ask casually, hoping he might say something about Spence.

"Oh, the work piles up and Ivan, the mad scientist, dashes around. One of these years I'm going to make a robot with somebody's brain inside, to do some of my work."

"Ugh. Ivan, I wish you wouldn't say those things."

He laughed. "Darling," he said, in a guttural voice, "why don't you come up to my lab and see me sometime?"

"Absolutely not," she said.

"Well, if you're going to stand in the way of scientific progress—"

He could go on like that for hours. She talked and laughed with him a while, but after she had hung up she felt empty and dissatisfied. Ivan was good fun and she enjoyed him. But at this stage, she was not interested in platonic friendships.

Spence did not call. She did not know whether to feel disappointed or relieved. She had told him not to call. He was married. It was foolish to go on seeing him. Ivan was not married. Ivan was witty, intelligent, considerate, good fun. Maybe she could become interested in Ivan. Maybe she was missing the nearby trees for looking at the forest.

On Saturday she wore a low-cut short black formal with a rhinestone pendant and long, glittering, rhinestone earrings. Ivan whistled upon seeing her and expressed proper admiration.

"Kate, you're downright glamorous. I was going to take you to a bar for beer and a sandwich, but this calls for quick upgrading of my strategy."

She laughed at him uncertainly. He just might have planned that. They went to the restaurant to which Spence had taken her last week. She felt a reluctance to go in but firmly repressed it. No use being silly.

When the waiter showed them to a reserved table she was reassured. Ivan had been kidding again. She was never quite sure when he was kidding.

During dinner, they talked about the ballet, which was to be performed by a touring group. East Burnham, although a large enough city, did not have its own company.

Ivan had seen the reviews. "You'll want to notice the *Firebird* part particularly," he said. "That's supposed to be something extra-special. A new girl, very sensational. When I saw the company in New York last winter, she was in the neophyte class. Shot right up since then."

He could discuss music and ballet and theatre with interest and intelligence. Kate had had many dates with him for concerts, ballets, plays, a couple of opera performances. She knew his thoughts about modern art, existentialism, and Camus. But in all this time, she felt she had not come to know Ivan himself.

She had never seen him express emotion over a friend or relative. Was he simply a cold-blooded intellectual, she wondered. No, you couldn't call him cold-blooded, exactly. His eyes lit up and his hands moved and his voice had warmth when he discussed ideas, experiences.

She watched his face as he talked. What was he really like? Or was this all there was to Ivan, the "mad" scientist, the wary bachelor, the platonic friend?

"—don't you think so?" said Ivan.

"Oh, yes, of course," she replied quickly, dragging her attention back to what he said.

He shook his head at her. "Kate, my lovely, your mind is miles away. I just said I love those stupid horror movies made to thrill moronic teenagers. I said I think they are the hope of the future. And you agreed."

She blushed. "So my mind drifted. And you had to experiment, darn you!"

He laughed, his dark eyes shining. "You'll be forgiven if you tell me exactly what your thoughts were."

She looked at him, tempted to tell the truth. "All right. I was wondering what you were really like. I know what you talk about. I know what your work is like. But I've never had the least glimpse of what emotions you feel, what moves you deeply, what you love or hate."

He blinked and a veil seemed to hide his eyes. "So that's what was on your mind. Why?"

She hesitated. He was a wary bachelor. No use scaring him to death, she thought wryly. "Oh, I've been thinking lately how few people I know—really know. No one at work, since Molly and Ted left. My folks live far away. Possibly you're a friend—but you must admit, I don't know you very well."

The waiter came with the check. The subject was dropped and Kate made no effort to pick it up again.

The ballet was good, especially the excerpt from *Firebird*. They discussed it in the lobby, during intermission, while Ivan had a cigarette. She watched the people as they went past, noticing they were all strangers. East Burnham was large, but not that large. One would think she would see at least two or three people she knew.

It made her feel a bit panicky, as in those occasional nightmares she had, during which she wandered alone and lost in the snow, searching for someone. The snow? Alaska, of course. Had the lonely feeling begun there, when she had learned with a child's surprise and shock that her revered father was quarreling with her beloved mother? Was that when she had begun to feel lost?

"There's the bell. We might as well drift back," said Ivan. He put his hand under her arm to guide her through the crowd. She saw men gaze at her as she went by. They looked. They made no effort to get to know her, even at the office. Why? Did she seem cold and uninteresting?

Spence had looked, and wanted, and taken. That was the difference. Listening to the first bars of music for the opening of the final ballet, she remembered the way Spence's hands had felt on her, his body moving powerfully, his deep voice in her ears, "Kate—Kate, you're so wonderful..."

She clenched her hands into tight fists, staring blindly at the colorful pageantry on the stage.

After the ballet, Ivan suggested dancing. "There's something about watching a ballet that makes me feel ridiculously competent. I could kick up my heels and swing you over the chandeliers. I'm sure of it."

She pretended to hesitate in alarm. "If you feel that way, I'd better go home!"

"Aw, come on. Live dangerously. What have you got to lose but a leg or an arm?"

So they went dancing. The orchestra was good. Ivan was amusing. But he did not try to make a spectacle of them on the dance floor. He was a good dancer, not holding her too close, but with an appreciation of the rhythm. She enjoyed the evening and almost forgot Spence.

When Ivan took her home, he said in the car, "What you were saying about emotions?"

She held her breath. "I've never fathomed yours." She was startled that he had brought up the subject.

"Well, my parents were divorced when I was seven. My mother had run off with another man. I lived with Dad till he was killed in an explosion at his plant. I was eleven. My uncle took me in. He was a bachelor. He didn't like scenes."

"Oh. I see."

"I learned I got ahead with him on brainpower. Nothing else." Ivan gave her a tight humorless grin. "You have to have lots of practice to feel emotions. I haven't loved anyone since mother left. Pretty late to start, isn't it?"

"Oh, Ivan. No, it isn't. You're missing so much." Her warm heart went out to him. "If I'd only known, I wouldn't have said—"

"You're a sweet kid." He pulled up in front of her apartment building and went around to open the door. She got out, walked to the door with him.

"Would you like to come up for some coffee or brandy?" she suggested, not wanting to seem unkind.

"Say, did you ever mix them? Quite a combination. Best is one pony brandy to one cup of coffee ... Naw, Kate, I won't come up. It's late and you ought to be tired. I tried hard enough to tire you out."

She smiled. He had on his clown mask again—Ivan, the mad scientist.

"All right, Ivan. I enjoyed it a lot. Thanks very much for asking me."

"We'll do it again one of these weeks."

He whistled as he walked back to the car. She took the elevator up to her apartment. So Ivan was as lost behind a mask as she was. Too bad. He was a nice guy.

In the apartment, she kicked off her shoes and put on bedroom slippers. She was too keyed up to sleep. She turned the radio to soft music, listened until she was relaxed. She could see ballet figures on her closed eyelids. Whenever she went to a ballet, afterward she could see the figures whirling on and on for hours.

She took a long hot shower and went to bed. She was close to sleep when she turned and reached out to touch someone. "Spence," she murmured sleepily.

The sound of her own voice wakened her. Her arm was feeling blindly for a form that was not there.

She lay awake, trying not to think of Spence, trying not to remember him. His mouth, hot and eager on her lips. His rough cheek against her shoulder, her breasts. His hands on her waist, on her thighs, under her back. She stiffened in the darkness. She could feel his hands on her. The feeling was so real, so vivid. But he was not there.

He was with his wife. Kate had been a brief affair, a quick fling. He was a man of strong desires, quick passions. He had wanted her, taken her, then forgotten her. That was all. And now it was over.

She would be smart to forget him as soon as possible. Maybe Ivan Todd could help her forget. He needed love, probably wanted love without knowing how to go about getting it. Maybe she and Ivan could help each other.

But she wanted Spence, his arms, his body, his voice, his presence...

CHAPTER SIX

S PENCE HAWK leaned back in his swivel chair and rubbed his eyes wearily. The figures in the drawings were blurred and indistinct. He could not concentrate on his work. His personal life kept intruding.

Leila. Demanding so much and giving so little, and that grudgingly. She did not love him and she never had. She frankly admitted she had been tired of working for a living, and had decided that being a wife would be a lot easier.

She was cheating on him with A. E. Pritchard, with others. She was thrill-hungry. He doubted if one man could satisfy her for long.

What a difference it would make, thought Spence, if a man could see into the future and find out what grief a woman would bring him before he ever took the risk of marrying her. Women wore such masks, they play-acted so expertly, that a man could be fooled into believing a woman was everything he had ever desired. Then—whambo! After the marriage the roof fell in.

He took a pipe from the rack, examined it absently, filled it, lit it. A blue cloud curled up from the pipe, and he leaned back to relax and enjoy the smoke. He must forget about Leila and get down to work.

His eyes went to the desk, to Reed's drawings.

Melvin Reed was doing pretty well, but he had a lot to learn. His book-knowledge was no substitute for practical experience. Spence examined the top drawing again, and groaned. It was beautiful, simply magnificent. The only trouble was that manufacturing this one part alone would cost about twice what the entire product ought to cost.

"How do you like it, Spence?" Melvin put his head in the door with timid eagerness.

"Come in, Melvin. Sit down." The lanky young man managed to stumble over a dictaphone cord before he fell into the hard chair opposite Spence's desk.

"This drawing—" Spence began, then happened to catch the eager, puppy-earnest stare of Melvin's brown eyes. Spence swallowed. "It's beautifully done," he said, more gently. "The trouble is your costs would be prohibitive."

"Oh!" Melvin looked like a slapped child. "I'm sorry—I'm awfully sorry. I didn't think of cost at all."

"That's the difference between scientific theory in a college lab, and practical experience in a company lab. But don't feel badly. You have a lot to learn about business, but you have a solid background of knowledge and training."

Melvin sighed. "I don't know why you ever hired me, much less made me your assistant," he said with childlike bluntness that reminded Spence of Kate. "You have to take more time to train me than it would take to do the work yourself."

"I'm thinking of the future," said Spence, not denying the charge. "The business is growing so fast I can scarcely keep up now. If I don't train a man now, I'll be out on a limb within a couple of years."

"I sure appreciate your taking the time to school me," said Melvin. "With Jennie having a baby and all—" His lean young face glowed. "It's to be in April, you know."

"Yes. That's great," said Spence, while a heavy pang of jealousy hurt his heart. A baby. This young kid was going to have a baby. His young wife wanted a child. And Spence was thirty-three, and didn't have a hope of getting a child from Leila.

"I was working on something else today," Melvin said. "I—well—I hardly know what you'll say. But you know how Ivan is fretting about the condensers? And Mr. Prichard's project about the motor—Mr. Roy Prichard, I mean. Well, I had an idea—I don't know—maybe it's goofy—" Awkwardly, he fumbled with a folder he had brought with him. He managed to extract a paper and handed it to Spence.

Spence took it and turned on the desk lamp to examine it more closely. He glanced at the sketch, not really expecting much. They had all fiddled with this problem for many months, now. Melvin could hardly be expected to turn up a solution ... then a detail caught Spence's eye.

"Well—say!" he blurted. "This looks good. That's a new idea."

Melvin beamed excitedly. "I don't know if it will work. But I thought of connecting it on the side instead of end to end. That makes it compact. Now if it will just work ... Do you think it might work, huh, Spence?"

Spence scarcely heard him, studying the drawing, picturing the finished product with half-closed eyes. The side-gimmick had been tried once, but the soldering had been such a problem they had given up on it. This arrangement of Melvin's would require less soldering.

"It looks good, Melvin. Darn good. I'll study it tonight and talk about it to Ivan tomorrow."

Melvin gave a great puff of relief. "Gee—I'm glad. Maybe I'll earn my pay this month."

Spence laughed at him kindly. "Don't ever worry about that, kid. You're worth it every month. And this is a smart idea. Listen, keep it under your hat. Don't talk about it to anyone."

Melvin's eyes grew round. "Spies?" he gasped.

"Could be," said Spence dryly. "It's been known to happen when competition gets rough. But I mean anyone around here. Let Ivan and me handle it for a while."

"Oh. Well, Cecil was asking me a few days ago what I was working on, and I told him. Is that okay?"

Melvin had not been here long enough to realize that interoffice tensions were bitter. "Does Cecil know about your solution?" Spence tapped the paper.

"No, I hadn't figured it out. I told him I thought we'd have to keep on with the older-type mechanism."

"Good. Leave it at that till I can talk to Roy and Ivan gets a chance to work out some models of this."

"Sure, Spence. Whatever you say." Melvin got up to leave, and knocked his chair backward. It crashed to the floor before he could catch it. "Gosh, I'm sorry. I'd best get out before I break up your whole office."

Spence grinned after him. Melvin was a good-hearted kid, and there was nothing wrong with his brain. It was just his nervous body that betrayed him at times. At the door, Bertha coming in dodged aside just in time to avoid a collision with Melvin going out.

"Gosh—Mrs. Foster!" stammered Melvin. "I didn't see you."

"It's all right, Melvin," she said with weary patience. "May I come in, Spence?"

He stood up. She closed the door after the departing Melvin.

"Is that boy capable of anything besides crashing into people?" she asked.

"He is. He has an excellent mind."

"I'm so happy to hear that." Bertha sat down. He offered her the box of cigarettes on his desk. There were heavy marks under her eyes, like dark bruises—the trophies of many sleepless nights, Spence guessed. "I've been wanting to talk to you about the meeting a couple of weeks ago. I finally read some carbons of letters." She smiled, mirthlessly. "To be honest, we were invited to Cecil's for dinner and while my dear brothers were drinking, I rifled Cecil's private files. I'm sure they're planning to price-fix operations. One letter was about the percentage of contracts to be awarded to each company. Cecil was holding out for twenty-three per cent instead of the nineteen offered."

"So it's gone that far?"

"Yes. I think they're planning another meeting. When are the bids due on the Air Force small motors?"

"Not till spring—late March or early April. We're still ironing out bugs in our proposed motor."

"They may be planning to rig bids on some other contracts, then. Cecil and A. E. are going to Florida in February."

"Florida? What's suspicious about that?"

"They have invited their wives to go along," said Bertha with sarcastic significance. "If it were a pleasure trip, they'd leave the girls at home."

Spence grimaced. Cecil and A. E. were notorious for their affairs. He wondered why their wives hadn't divorced them. Those women, he thought, must love money to put up with such humiliation.

Bertha fumbled with her handbag, got out her lipstick and repaired her mouth. "Gilbert asked me to go, too," she said, finally.

"Will you?"

"I don't know what to do. I think he's buttering me up because I won't sign new proxies."

Spence was silent. He did not know what to advise.

"If I went, I might get some idea what they're up to," suggested Bertha. She put away the lipstick. Her mouth was a bright unattractive orange, to match her orange suit. It was a mistake for her to try to appear twenty-five, thought Spence. She was a fine-looking woman of forty-two. "And maybe Gil and I could patch things up. He's really not a bad guy, you know. He just gets big ideas now and then, a sort of power complex."

"Sure," said Spence. Poor Bertha, he thought. Would she never learn?

"I think I'll go. And keep an eye on the boys."

"And get a nice tan," said Spence.

"Do you think I'm going to put on a bathing suit and lie out in the sun beside the teenagers? Hell, no. I always was sensitive about my skinny body." She laughed self-consciously, and stood up. "I'll stay in the smoke-filled rooms."

Spence stood also. He wanted to warn Bertha, yet not hurt her. "Bertha," he said finally, "don't sell yourself short. You're a wonderful woman."

Her mouth trembled as though she were going to cry. "How do you mean—sell myself short?" she asked.

"Don't let anyone—uh—trick you."

"Gilbert?" She stared at the gloves she was pulling nervously between her long fingers. "I wanted to believe his lies, Spence. But by this time I know they are lies. If I'm tricked, it will be because of moonlight, lies, and too much to drink." She closed the door after her.

Spence worked on. Later in the day he called Leila. "I'm going to stay in town this evening, Leila. Too much work."

He expected an outburst of anger. She surprised him. "Oh, darling, again?" She cooed sweetly, "You're working yourself to death. Aren't you coming home at all tonight?"

"Yes, but it may be close to midnight."

"All right, sweetheart."

He hung up, frowning. When Leila was sweet, she was up to her neck in trouble. He returned to his labors for a while, concentrating on Melvin's projects, drawing them again from various angles. But he could not stay concentrated. He kept wondering what Leila was up to.

About eight o'clock he gave up and drove home. Upper Dales was a suburb of East Burnham, developed by an enterprising real estate firm within a three-year period. All the houses were either split-level or tri-level, all had large lots around them, all were expensive, imitative and undistinguished. On street after street, the same house plans were repeated with monotonous precision, some in brick, some wood, some stone, but all bland-faced, picture-windowed, closely manicured. Few trees remained. There were only small bushes, a few tiny flower plots, "so the friendly feeling isn't ruined by fences," the salesman had explained with great enthusiasm.

Spence's house was dark except for a light in the bedroom, shining through the drawn curtains. Leila in bed at this hour? Was she reading? Not likely. On impulse, Spense drove on past his house, drove around the block, and parked near several other cars in front of a house where a party was in progress. Before he got out of the car, he located the key to the back door on his key chain. The back door was farther from the bedroom windows.

He walked quietly around the house and let himself in. The house was still.

He walked through the kitchen, to the family room. Family. His mouth curled. His family room had witnessed parties that would make a real family run away screaming.

He walked up the stairs slowly, glad of the thick runner that silenced his footsteps. The bedroom door was partly open, a light shone out. As he drew closer, he heard Leila's voice.

"Sweet—honey—go on—go on—again. Oh—sweet—"

Spence pushed open the door and stood watching for a minute. They did not notice him. His wife was lying naked on their bed, sprawled out beside the active tanned body of a man. As Spence gazed, he saw the man move with practiced precision, and sink down on the lush white body. White legs came up to grip him, white arms banded his torso.

The man's head turned as he kissed Leila's white shoulder and arm. Spence saw his face and recognized Earl Kennard, the Army lieutenant who had moved into Upper Dales a month before.

"Leila!" Spence roared. Leila's body jerked. Her face came up. Her blue eyes were glazed.

"Oh—Spence—" she sighed languidly. She made no move to push the man away.

Kennard's head raised alertly. He looked at Spence specu-
latively. But he was not alarmed either. Evidently he felt certain
enough of Leila's cooperation not to fear Spence; he made no
effort to disengage himself from Spence's wife.

For some reason that made Spence furious. He had half
expected to find someone in bed with Leila. But now these people
did not even act guilty. It was as if Spence were the interloper,
breaking illicitly into the bedroom of two lovers and interrupt-
ing their pleasure.

He strode over to the bed, grabbed Kennard's arm and pulled.
Leila shrieked and sat up. The two separated, and Kennard sprang
erect, bounding off the bed and striking at Spence.

Spence struck back. He felt Kennard's fist on his chin, sliding
to graze his cheek. The man was lithe and tough, a fact which
Spence welcomed. He had been wanting to fight something, or
someone, for a long time.

Spence slugged Kennard hard in the chest. The man staggered back, recovered, came at Spence again. Spence's heavy suit
and topcoat hindered his movements. The other man was stark
naked and active as a dancer. He weaved like a trained boxer,
feinted with his right, then his left struck like a snake and con-
nected with Spence's jaw. Spence's head snapped back with a
painful jolt.

Spence was hit again in the nose. Blood spurted. He was dis-
tracted by the swift flow of blood. He tried to hit Kennard again,
but the man ducked. Spence concentrated like a drunk on the
weaving figure before him, grabbed him in heavy arms and flung
him to the floor.

Leila screamed, and yelled, "Stop that! Spence, you let him
alone! Spence, get away from him!"

Kennard seemed spent. Sprawled on the floor, Spence figured the breath had been knocked out of the man. Spence
found a handkerchief and held it to his nose, and glared down
at Kennard. The soldier got to his knees, ready to spring again.

"Get out," said Spence roughly. "Get your clothes and get out."

The other man eyed him curiously. "Okay," he said nonchalantly.

Spence followed him to the top of the stairs, watched him go down.

Spence went to the bathroom, soaked a towel in cold water and held it at the back of his neck. When the bleeding stopped, he cleaned up and took off his topcoat. He went downstairs, made sure Kennard had left, locked up and went up to undress in the guest bed, smoking for a while, unable to calm down.

Finally he went to the other bedroom. Leila pretended to be asleep, huddled down under the covers. Spence snapped on the light, pulled the covers off Leila and looked at her.

"Spence, honey, come to bed," she said, opening wary blue eyes.

He sat down at her side. She smiled and moved over. He caught her up roughly, spun her across his knees, and pulled up the flimsy nightdress she was now wearing.

"Spence!" she shrieked. "Don't you dare! I'll hate you forever—"

"You've been asking for this for a long time," he said grimly. He raised his hand high and let it come down on her plump hips with a hard, satisfying smack. She shrieked louder. He spanked her again and again. She cried and begged. He hit her harder and harder till his hand was tired. She wriggled and cursed him and threatened him.

"I'll pay you back for this," she wept. "I'll pay you! I'll pay—"

He sent one last blow to her rump, then pushed her away from him.

"Spence," she sobbed as he left the room. "*Spence—*"

He slammed the door, went to the guest room and locked himself in. He wouldn't have put it past her to come to him in bed. She was a complex devil and she would do anything to get her way.

He fell asleep, sprawled across the mattress, tired, frustrated, angry, helpless. There was nothing that he could do that would change Leila into the kind of wife he wanted.

CHAPTER SEVEN

EILA was sullenly angry at Spence for several days. By the end of the week he was eating all his meals in town to stay out of her way.

His own anger had died, leaving him resigned and contrite. After all, his own record was not clean. He had slept with another woman, and had thoroughly enjoyed it.

His marriage was on the rocks, but it was partly his own fault. He had not meant for things to work out this way. And Leila could be sweet and lovable when she wanted to be.

If she would only get her fill of adultery and sexual calesthenics. Surely she would get fed up with them one day. Then she might settle down, have at least one child, and help him establish a real home. There was no future in the empty life they were leading.

He tried to say that to Leila on Saturday. She was still angry at him.

"You had no right to spank me like that. I'm still sore." She rubbed her bottom accusingly.

"I've said I'm sorry. You shouldn't have had that guy in here."

"If it's all right at a party, why isn't it all right at home?"

That was unanswerable. She knew that. The only logical conclusion was that their neighborhood parties were not "all right."

These parties were inclined to get pretty sexy. They were attended only by a select circle, known as "the club." A certain amount of wife-swapping was considered the smart thing and more than once, urged on by Leila, he had succumbed to temptation, allowing her to do the same.

"I don't want you bringing men home, that's all," said Spence wearily.

Leila had a voice that went up easily to a shrill pitch that rang through his aching head. "Spence, you've gotten so stuffy! What's the matter with you?"

"Getting old," he said grimly.

She turned to solicitude. "You poor darling, you're all tired out. You work too hard. All work and no play makes Spence a dull husband." She pushed him down on the couch and sat on his lap and said loving things to him. She could be sweet.

He ruffled up her long blond hair, and she did not reproach him. He sighed. Maybe if he played along with her, went to the parties cheerfully, saw she had a good time, took her out more, she would be more satisfied, and not run off to men like Kennard and A. E. Pritchard.

"You do work too hard," Leila said in his ear, rubbing her warm cheek against his rough one. "No wonder you growl like a bear. You need fun."

He stroked his hand along her lithe back to the plump hips. "Do you want to go out tonight? Go dancing?" He meant just the two of them.

"Oh, darling, I do want to," she said happily. "But the Thorntons are throwing a party tonight and everybody's going."

He groaned. "Oh, Leila, not that gang—"

She pouted, then pressed her luscious red mouth to his. "Please, sweet. You'll love it. You always do when the party gets going. And Peggy Kennard is quite a dish! You haven't seen her yet, have you?"

"Earl Kennard's wife?"

"Yes." Leila watched him out of narrowed blue eyes. "She's been around. They've been stationed everywhere, and the things she knows—wow! Leon is real crazy about her."

Leon Thornton and his wife Amy were real crazy, period, Spence mentally amended. He sometimes thought Leila would not have such wild ideas if she were not such a friend of Amy's. The Thorntons were an arty, exotic couple who had taken over the Upper Dales set when they had moved in a year ago.

"Why don't we go out by ourselves for a change?" he said. "There's a new orchestra at the Grand. You used to like to dance—"

"Oh, Spence! You never want to do what I want. You haven't gone to any parties with me since before Christmas." She pouted at him and kissed him and snuggled up to him. "Besides, you'll like Peggy. And you can take her away from Leon just like that. She'll really go for you."

In spite of himself, Spence was interested. He must be as depraved as the rest of them, he thought ruefully, as he showered and dressed for the party. He was curious to meet Peggy. Maybe if he made up to her, Leila might get jealous enough to break off from the crowd. If not—Peggy herself probably would be sufficient reward. And one of these years, Leila would get fed up. She developed sudden enthusiasms about people but she dropped them fast enough when she became bored. All he could do was hold the marriage together with glue until she was ready to settle down.

They were late reaching the Thorntons' because Leila liked to arrive late, after things had warmed up. She hated cold parties. So it was past ten when Spence rang the doorbell.

George Winter opened the door, glass in hand. "Come in. Glad to see you, Spence. Where have you been?"

"Working," Spence said briefly.

"Close the door," a woman screamed. "I'm freezing!"

Several men laughed. "I'll warm you, Peggy. Come on over!"

Spence and Leila left their coats on a hall rack and went into the darkened living room. The hi-fi was playing Pacific Island native dances, one of Leon's favorite records. Two women were dancing in the middle of the room, red and orange spotlights flickering over them. They postured and contorted, deliberately provocative. Both were very drunk.

Spence was staring at the women. He had seen Amy before. The other must be Peggy Kennard. She had long black curly hair, a sleek white body with high pointed breasts, wide hips, long graceful legs. As he watched, she pulled her skirt to her waist, leaped in the air, then sank to the floor in a perfect split. The men applauded.

"Like a drink?" said George. Leon, the host, was putting another record on the player.

Spence tore his gaze from the women and then followed George to the bar.

"It's going to be a hot night," said George, opening his collar. He was older than the others, about forty-five. His face was heavily flushed. He glanced toward his wife, LaVerne, who was sitting on someone's lap in a big chair. "Real hot," he said again, turning back to the bar.

It was one of the rules of the crowd that no one could object to whatever his wife or her husband did during a party.

"Let's play strip poker," Jim McClure suggested. He was holding LaVerne.

Peggy Kennard objected. "What fun is that? Somebody dance—like I did," she said, flexing her attractive body.

"Right," cried Leila, and caught Earl's hand. She drew him into the spotlights with her. "Come on, baby, let's dance!"

The others yelled and cheered as Leila and Earl began to dance to the rhythmic insinuating music. Earl unzipped the dress at Leila's back, then stripped it down to her shoulders. She unfastened his tie, the buttons on his shirt. They were laughing, gazing at each other.

Spence watched them moodily, his second glass in his hand. They started to embrace right there on the floor but Amy Thornton stopped them.

"Not yet, kids. Save it!" she said. "We're going to play some games first. We'll start with musical chairs."

They all liked that game. Leon counted the couples—six—and put six records on the player. A couple of the fellows put six chairs in the middle of the room, three with backs to the other three. By that time the other three girls—LaVerne, Gail McClure, and Sharon Young—were getting as drunk as Peggy.

Spence, too, had had enough to drink by that time to try to get in the spirit of the thing. All the men then sat down in the chairs, and a girl sat down on each lap.

Spence got Gail McClure the first time. She was sweet and she liked him. As the music started, he pulled her back on his lap, and hugged her, and kissed her shoulders. George next to him was having trouble with Peggy. She wriggled and giggled and sat forward on his knees so he hardly had a chance to kiss her.

The music stopped. The girls jumped up. George pulled away his chair and went over to stand at the bar. The girls ran around shrieking, each trying to get a man's lap. Five girls made it. Sharon Young was out, so she went to stand beside George at the bar.

Spence got LaVerne. He was beginning to get excited, and she was young, a lot younger than her husband, George, and full of ginger. She gave him a rough time, which excited him the more. Then the music stopped.

Fred Young pulled out next. He usually stopped when his wife did. Spence figured Fred and Sharon were about the only ones in the gang who really cared for each other.

The girls ran around, fighting over the remaining men. Spence saw his chance and grabbed Peggy. He pulled her down hard on his lap.

Gail retired to the sidelines to watch.

"You've been avoiding me," Spence told Peggy.

She looked at him over her bare shoulder, provocatively. Her hips wriggled as she settled herself more comfortably.

"You're a pretty rough guy. You scare me," she said.

He grinned. She was referring, of course, to his fist-fight with her husband. She stopped moving for a moment. He drew her back sharply. He had learned a lot about this game in the past year.

Peggy gasped.

All too soon the music stopped. She shot out of his lap like a wounded rabbit. He grinned to see her go, stood up and pulled his chair to the sidelines. He felt as if he had got a bit of revenge on the lieutenant.

Leila sidled up to Spence as he stood at the bar. "How was she, Spence?"

Leila's face was heavily flushed, her eyes unnaturally bright. She must have been pouring down the drinks.

"Interesting," he said briefly.

"Told you so." Leila laughed. When the game stopped, she danced over to Leon Thornton's chair, and plunked herself down on his lap.

Spence went to the kitchen for a glass of cold water. The house was hot, the way Amy Thornton liked it for one of these parties. He opened the kitchen curtain and stared out at the snowy white world. It must have started snowing soon after they arrived. Now the ground was covered, and the roofs of houses, and the limbs of the bare trees.

"Spence? Here you are." It was Amy's sultry voice. "Are you hiding out on us?" She padded over to him on her bare feet, and put her hands against his chest. Her dark eyes studied him wisely.

He watched her as he sipped the cold water. There was something he wanted to know, and he figured he could get the information from Amy.

He set down the glass, put his hands lightly on her back, drew her close. She snuggled up to him.

He said, "It's been a long time."

"You haven't been around," she reproached.

"You're the one always missing—running off to New York with Leila." He worked his hands over her carefully in the way that he remembered drove her crazy. He leaned back against the sink and braced himself. She put her arms around his neck, and lifted a knee toward his waist. He pulled her closer, and made her wait, putting his fingers deep into her.

"Come on Spence, honey." She lifted herself higher on him.

"Leila says you both had a great time in New York."

"Great. Sure. At least she did."

"With A. E. Pritchard, huh?" he said casually. "He's quite a spender."

"Yeah, when you can get him out of bed!" blurted Amy. "Honestly, I went more places alone—"

He knew what he wanted to know. A. E. and Leila had spent the whole time together. "Didn't you have any boy friends to keep you happy?"

"Oh, A. E. found one—" Then she stopped. Her brain, dulled by liquor, functioned slowly. "Say, who said A. E. was there at all?"

"Wasn't he?"

"No. 'Course not. That must have been some other time. Some other guy, I mean. Leila and I just wandered around. Had fun."

She was a poor liar. The fact that she even bothered to try meant that Leila must have warned her to keep her mouth shut about A. E.

The sink hurt his back. He stood erect, moved Amy over to a chair. He sat down, pulled her on his lap. She faced him, put her head down on his shoulder, and got in place expertly. Even drunk, Amy could make all the right sex moves. He let her use him for her satisfaction. It took little time.

The kitchen door opened. Earl and Leila peered in. "Oh, there you are, Spence," said Leila. "I knew you'd have fun once you got here. It's the hardest thing to drag him to a party," she said to Earl. "You wouldn't believe how hard it is."

"But he does have fun," said Earl, mockingly, watching Amy as she got off Spence's knees. "Doesn't he, Amy?"

"I have the fun. Spence is the most. The top most," sighed Amy. She looked at him. "Thanks sweetie. You're the greatest."

Earl stopped grinning. "I thought you said I was," he said to Amy.

"Sweet, you're all right. But Spence is the most."

Spence felt lost in a lunatic world. The only reality was the stark, bitter jealousy on Earl's face, the amusement on Leila's.

This was all wrong, this rutting, this casual coupling in corners. And not on moral grounds alone. Sex itself lost all meaning when it was taken lightly; the value was out of it, the pleasure was thin.

"Well, back to the party," said Amy, patting her black curly hair. "Who knows a new game?"

They returned to the living room. Fred and Sharon Young, Leon and Peggy, Gail McClure and George Winter, all were dancing. Jim McClure and LaVerne Winter were missing, but soon showed up—Jim looking rather sheepish.

"We'd better get on home," said George Winter hopefully. "It's after midnight."

"Don't be a wet blanket," LaVerne told him crossly.

Spence figured Jim had just disappointed her and she was not yet ready to go. She eyed Earl hopefully but he was absorbed with Leila. She, however, was occupied with Leon. He put his arms around her, and patted her plump hips, but he was looking toward Peggy.

A foolish bunch of hopeful lovers, Spence mused. He sat down in a big chair and watched. George loved LaVerne. LaVerne wanted Earl, Earl wanted Leila, Leila wanted Leon. Dead end there.

Gail McClure came over and perched on the arm of Spence's chair. "Hi," she said.

"Hi, Gail, honey," he said. He liked Gail and Jim. They were a pretty nice couple. "Having fun?"

"Not much," she said. He followed her gaze to Peggy and Amy, beginning another dance in the center of the room. All the men were watching them. Even Leila was neglected, and sat pouting sullenly.

"They get the spotlight," said Spence as Fred flicked off the room lights and centered spots on the two writhing figures. Leon got his bongo drums and started beating out the rhythm.

"And the men," said Gail. Her fingers trailed along Spence's shoulder.

He took the hint and drew her down on his lap. It was dark in the corner, and Gail was sweet. And he felt lost and crazy and mixed up, and the drinks were fuzzing his mind. Nothing made sense.

The girls danced, and he held Gail close. She was a little different from the others. She was sweet and gentle, so he took no liberties, just held her and enjoyed the warmth and softness of her. He could tell that she was frightened, too.

"I can hear your heart beating like a little rabbit," he said, his head on her breast.

Her breath was coming fast. "Oh, Spence. Yes, I am frightened, but—would you—I mean ..."

He smiled at her. He liked to look at her. She had corn yellow hair and blue eyes and a baby skin, and her heartbeat pulsed at her throat. He liked the way her soft breasts moved to her fast breathing.

"All right," he said. "If you're sure."

"I'm sure."

They left the others, found a bedroom. She would not let him put on a light. In the darkness, she came to him on the bed.

"You're sweet, Spence," she whispered. "You're nice."

They came together in a warm passion that built up to a hot frenzy. He soon realized she was unable to find completion on her own, and gently took charge. She lay quiet in his arms as he deftly helped her.

She crumpled up under him, and cried out, and he felt the shivering of her. He let himself go then, and escaped just in time. He did not want anything to happen to her and she was the kind of girl who did not know all the precautions.

While he lay there, he felt her stir. She turned her head and kissed him.

"Thanks, Spence, for being so sweet."

"The pleasure was mine."

"Spence, may I ask you something?"

"Sure, Gail. Shoot."

"When Jim makes love to me, I—I don't feel anything. When you do, I feel—wonderful. But I don't love you. I love him."

"It's only a matter of technique." Spence felt uncomfortable.

"We joined the club because Jim wanted to know more about women, you see. And it worked—sort of. But he still can't—" She fell silent.

Spence sat up. "I'll have to talk with Jim some time. Okay?" He did not want to, but these were nice kids. "And there are books."

"We read some, but they didn't help." She slid off the bed. "I'm sorry I bothered you with it, Spence."

"Nonsense." He caught her arm, drew her back, kissed her. "Don't worry. And learn to relax and enjoy it. That helps as much as anything. Two nervous people don't have fun."

"Oh. Really?"

"Really." He kissed her shoulder. "I could feel how nervous you were. So I waited till you relaxed. Then—zoom. Everything was fine."

They went back to the living room. Sharon Young was being held by Leon, while Earl was trying to embrace her. The girls were watching, rather uneasily, Spence thought.

George Winter was saying, "But she doesn't want to! Don't!"

Earl laughed. He bent over. Sharon writhed, her eyes large and frightened.

Fred Young snarled, "Let her go."

Peggy held him from interfering. "Oh, shut up! Earl's good. Let him."

"What's going on?" Spence demanded.

"Oh, I don't want—don't—" said Sharon feebly. Leon held her as she struggled, watching her face with what Spence realized was sadistic enjoyment.

That was enough for Spence. He pulled Earl away by main force and knocked him down.

"Rule number one. Nobody does anything they don't want to. Remember?" said Spence. Earl warily got up from the floor.

Leon still held Sharon. "Listen, she'll like it—"

Spence hit him on the jaw. Leon's hands flew up and he staggered to the wall.

Now Earl was up and rushing at Spence. But the soldier was so drunk he staggered. Spence knocked him down again. This time Earl lay still. Leila and Peggy shrieked and ran to help Earl.

Sharon was crying, clinging to Fred. "You'd better go home," Spence told them.

He left with them, a few minutes later. Leila preferred to remain. She would find somebody to get her back to the house, she assured Spence.

They waved. He waved.

He drove home slowly, the windows open to the cold, pure air. The snow had stopped, and there was a hush and beauty in the night that made him ache with pain and frustration and desire for something he couldn't name.

After he had put the car in the garage, he stood outside for a long time, looking at the ice heavy on the branches of the trees, and the snow piled like cotton on the evergreen bushes, and the shadows that lay blue on the white unmarred lawns and streets.

He was cold when he finally went inside, but he felt cleaner, cold and tired and empty and clean.

CHAPTER EIGHT

S PENCE slept in the guestroom that night, figuring Leila would come home drunk. But she did not come home at all till noon next day.

And she had a hangover, a red-eyed, sick-faced, killer of a hangover. She had slept a few hours at the Thorntons' after the rest of the gang had left, and she was cross, belligerent, angry at Spence.

"Why did you walk out on the party? Huh? Why did you?"

"I was sick of it," he said shortly.

"Yeah. After you had Peggy, and Amy, and Gail. Sure. After."

He couldn't deny that.

"What's the matter with you? Are you wearing out, getting old? Can't you take it?" she sneered.

"No, I can't take it."

She stumbled around the kitchen, her gay, red, party dress bedraggled, the zipper open halfway down her back, her limp blond hair hanging in her eyes. She found the coffeepot, but couldn't seem to co-ordinate her movements enough to make coffee. He watched her in pitying disgust, and finally made the coffee himself.

He made it strong and black. She drank two cups, thirstily, careless of how hot it was. He drank a few swallows, staring down at the top of the kitchen table, tracing a pattern with his spoon.

When she seemed more rational, he said, "Leila, I want to quit this gang. They aren't good for us."

"Good? Who the hell wants to be good? I want fun—fun—" Her voice rose on the last word and she waved her arms wildly in the air, then let them fall limply. "Oh, my head's killing me."

"It wouldn't be killing you if you hadn't had too much liquor and too much sex."

She squinted at him sardonically through reddened lids. "Look who's talking. Old down-the-hatch Spence. I've known you to make love to more than one woman in one night, and some of them twice."

He winced. "Yeah. I'm a killer. Sure." He wondered what Kate would have thought if she had seen him like that. She probably would have run away screaming.

"But I'm fed up, Leila. There's more to life than parties. I want kids—"

"Oh, crap! Not that old record! Play another tune, Spence, or I'll listen to someone else's record. I mean that."

"Like A. E.'s? You like his songs, don't you?"

"Sure. He's not afraid to spend money to have fun."

"The way you had fun with him in New York?"

"Sure." She shrugged, and poured another cup of coffee with unsteady hands, the long red-lacquered fingernails clacking against the china cup. "I don't care what you think any more, Spence. All you do is try to spoil my fun. I'm going to do what I please, from now on."

"I thought that's what you had been doing."

"Huh. It's just a little bit compared to what I will do." Her eyes were bright blue devils. "From here on out, you do what I say, or you'll be sorry!"

Was she still drunk? What had gotten into her? Spence eyed her with weary curiosity. "What do you mean by that?"

"You'll find out." She nodded at him with coy cunning. She would not talk till she was ready.

Well, bad news could always wait.

Spence tried again, without much heart for the job. "Look, Leila, things are in a mess between us. I don't want our marriage to crack up. Let's try again—really try."

"What do you want to do? Go to bed with me? And have a baby, huh?" Leila started to chuckle, drunkenly. "Oh, I see through you, Spence. You'd like me to have a kid! Sure. Then I'll have to stay home and be good, huh? You wouldn't have to worry about where I was, and who's in bed with me, huh?"

He tightened his mouth against her angry scorn. Why did he even try? She did not want an ordinary decent home, a child, a quiet, good life. She wanted parties, men, excitement, and fun—fun—fun.

"Well, let me tell you," said Leila, "I'm not going to get caught in any trap. I'm going to have—"

"Fun. I know." Spence got up and took his cup over to the sink to rinse it. "Well, you can go to those parties alone. I'm not going any more."

"Hah-hah-hah! Well, you won't have to go next Saturday. Everybody's coming here to our house! What do you think of that?"

He flung around. "You didn't invite them here?"

"Oh, yes, I did. It's our turn." She watched his face with brightly malicious satisfaction. "They're coming here. Amy and Leon, and Earl and Peggy, and George and LaVerne."

He stared at her. "What about Fred and Sharon?"

"They dropped out. So did Jim and Gail. Just as well. Fred and Jim are no good."

"You should know," commented Spence. But they're smart, getting out. I think this is a good time for us to get out, too."

"Not on your life!" Leila staggered to her feet, clutched the back of the chair to steady herself. "No, sir! Not little Leila."

She lurched out of the room and he heard her heels clatter on the stairs up to the bedroom.

The party would be here next week, the worst of the old gang.

No more, he thought. No more. He said it aloud: "No more. I'm through. No more."

If he could not talk Leila out of having the gang here, he would spend the weekend in town, he resolved. He could not face himself after another time like last evening. And he had no doubt that the gang would invent new games, new frantic dances, new frenzies to whip up their erotic natures.

Where would it end? Could he hope that Leila would eventually learn she was wasting herself, would get out when she woke up? Maybe. It might work out that way.

But it seemed pretty certain that Spence could not talk her out of her pleasures, right now. To her he was just a wet blanket, a spoil-sport, a cold fish.

The house grew quiet. Leila must have fallen asleep. Spence got his briefcase and spread out drawings on the dining-room table, and worked till the gray afternoon turned to dusk, and dusk turned to night.

At least, he had his work. He could forget, for a while, the frustrations of his personal life.

When Leila was completely sober again, she tried to coax Spence to join the crowd that weekend.

"You'll love it, Spence. You always do. And Peggy said you were terrific. She wants to see you again."

"No, thanks. No more, Leila."

"Come on. Don't be cross. I'm not mad at you, am I? You walked out, but I'm not mad. Come on, sweet. Just think—this is going to be loads of fun."

He hesitated. He was tempted. Maybe he was the queer one, to be repelled by sexual opportunity. Maybe it was normal to want one woman after another, to want to try them all. Maybe he was a fool to say no.

But he said it. "No, Leila. No more. If you're having a party, I'll stay in town."

He stuck by that in spite of her pleading and coaxing.

She finally said, "If you change your mind, come on back. Promise you'll come back if you change your mind. I'll miss you, darling. The party won't be the same."

Which was the real Leila? This sweet-voiced, lovable, desirable woman—or the sardonic, cruel, belligerent female with a hangover? He did not know.

He took a suitcase to work on Friday; enough clothes to last till Monday evening. Melvin Reed saw the suitcase in his office.

"Are you going on a trip, Spence?" he asked timidly.

"I'm not sure yet. I packed in case it's necessary."

"Oh. Here are the new drawings I told you about." He handed them over with shy transparent pride.

"Already? You must have worked all night on them."

Melvin blushed like a child. "Gee. Only a few hours. Jennie says I get inspired and have to work."

"These look great, Melvin. Really great. You're doing a swell job."

"Do you mean that?"

"I sure do." Spence felt funny because Melvin was doing a much better job than Spence had anticipated when he had hired the boy. All Melvin needed was some encouragement and direction. He had great possibilities.

When the time came to pack up Friday evening, Spence fought the temptation to go home to Upper Dales, help Leila get liquor and food for the party, give in to the frantic urges that motivated the suburbia set. Leon would bring records and his bongo drums. Peggy and Amy would do their sensuous dances, and the lights would play on their beautiful, writhing bodies. There would be bold invitations. He could run his hands over sleek thighs, hold a curved body against his, awaken passions, satisfy his own desires when and where he pleased.

He put off the decision by working late, then having a solitary dinner at a quiet restaurant. But finally he went to the car.

He had to drive somewhere—to a lonely, impersonal hotel or to his home in Upper Dales.

He drove aimlessly, a few miles, pretending he was looking for a hotel. He did not want to go home but he hated the thought of being alone. He was tired, empty, frustrated. He wanted to talk with someone pleasant, to listen to someone cheerful, to sleep with someone warm and gentle and receiving.

Ahead of him was the entrance to a private garage. It looked familiar. Then he realized it was the garage under the apartment building where Kate lived.

Without a second thought, he turned in, drove down the ramp and parked at the spot where he had before. There was a phone at the elevator door. He rang her apartment. Maybe she was not home, maybe she would not see him, maybe—

"Hello?" It was her soft, low voice.

"Kate. It's Spence."

"Oh! Where are you?"

"In the building garage. May I come up and see you?"

"Oh, yes. Yes!" There was no mistaking her eagerness. It made him bold.

"I brought my suitcase. I want to stay."

He heard her breath catch. "Oh. Yes, Spence."

She opened the door for him when he arrived upstairs. She looked serious, uncertain, questioning. She had said he wasn't to come back. But there was nowhere else to go, nowhere in the world he wanted to go.

He set down the suitcase. She closed the door. He shrugged out of his overcoat,

"I'll take it," she said. "It's wet. I'll hang it in the kitchen."

He followed her into the kitchen. He felt that he could never allow her out of his sight. She looked so beautiful, her hair shining and smooth in the French roll, her body rounded and full in a dark red wool dress.

She hung the overcoat on a chair and turned to face him. "Spence—" she began.

He did not wait for polite questions and polite answers. He took the step that separated them and drew her against him. His mouth sought hers hungrily.

She lifted her head and accepted his kiss. Her mouth was soft and full and parted and warm. He held her tight and satisfied his longing against her lips, kissing her long and hard. Then he kissed her cheeks and chin, the soft flesh below her ears, her mouth again.

"Oh, Kate! Kate," he said, at last. "Oh, Kate."

She put her warm hands on either cheek and looked at him long and soberly, her dark brown eyes studying his face.

"I thought you weren't coming back. I told you not to."

He smiled. He wanted to laugh and whistle and sing for joy. "I stayed away as long as I could. I had to come back."

Her fingers caressed his face. He kissed her hands, held them against his mouth. He studied her face greedily, with the interest of a wanderer who has returned after a long journey. Yes, her eyes were dark brown, with large irises. The eyebrows were dark wings. He smoothed a wing caressingly. There were hollows in her cheeks, and he had to touch them, and feel how soft her face was.

They went in the other room and sat on the couch, very close. Spence put his hand behind her neck and held her head so he could look at her face. His other hand caressed her arm under the loose, red wool sleeve.

"What have you been doing these weeks?" he asked, not because he had to know, but because he wanted her to speak and tell him about herself.

"Working overtime again. Not much else. I saw a couple of movies."

"Who did you go with?"

"I went alone."

A beautiful woman, a warm loving woman, going to movies alone. It was a crazy world. Men chased after hard, tough, artificial women like Leila and Peggy and Amy. But women like Kate walked alone. Was everyone both blind and stupid?

"What have you been doing?" she asked.

"Working overtime, also." He smiled a little. "Working on a new motor. I was planning on locking myself in a hotel room this weekend to do some drawing."

"You could work here. There's a card table," she said seriously.

"I believe you mean that."

"Of course."

"You'd let me stay all weekend, and you wouldn't mind if I worked?" Leila hated him to bring work home. It made her cross for him to concentrate for hours at a time on his "stupid papers."

"Of course, Spence. Why not?"

Why not, indeed?

"I can't believe you're real. Am I dreaming?"

"I could pinch you," she offered.

"Kiss me instead."

Her kiss was sweet and warm, and her arms came up around his neck. He moved his hand from her arm to her waist, down to her thigh, smoothed along her leg to her knee, up again. He could feel her warmth through the wool dress, her perfume was heady, and presently it was no longer enough to caress and kiss.

They went to her bedroom. This time he wanted to undress her, and insisted on taking off the red wool dress, the white slip, the fragile bits of underclothing. She blushed and protested. "Let me, Spence—I can—"

"I want to." He pulled her back into his arms and kissed her while he unfastened her brassiere and pulled the straps off her shoulders. He paused to play with her big full breasts, and tease her shyness while delighting in it. He pulled off the rest of her clothes, then made her stand before him so he could look at her.

She crossed her arms in front of her in a vain effort to hide herself.

"No. Put your arms down. Let me see you." Gently he drew her arms away from her body and looked. "You're beautiful, Kate. Don't hide yourself."

But she was self-conscious and troubled, so he let her go and she got in bed and pulled the covers to her shoulders. He turned out the lights and joined her.

She was stiff in his arms.

"Kate, are you angry?"

"No. I just—felt odd."

"You're beautiful. I wanted to see you."

"I know." Her arms went around his neck, her body relaxed slowly under his caressing hands. "I'm not used to—letting a man see—"

He had invaded her privacy so rudely and swiftly. She wasn't like Leila or any of the others, parading their nakedness in arrogance and lust.

"I'm sorry, Kate. Truly sorry."

"It's all right. I shouldn't be so prudish."

"No. I like that. I like being the only man—" He stopped, abruptly realizing that he had no right to say anything. This was only a casual affair, an extramarital fling. He was married. Kate was no more than a mistress for a few nights. He must not let himself get too deeply involved. That would mean trouble.

He said no more. His passion rose swiftly in the privacy and darkness of the comfortable bed. Soon she opened to him like a warm rose under the heat of the sun.

She was learning how to please him. Their desires increased, kept pace each with the other's, raced feverishly with their racing pulses.

He held her down as he reached consummation.

She was tired then. He could feel her tiredness in the limpness of her body. He wrapped his arms around her possessively tight. He didn't want to let her go. Still less did he want to get up and leave her. He wanted Kate again, but he wanted more for her to rest and lie quiet against his body, so he could touch her breasts as they rose and fell, touch her thighs as they moved slowly to a comfortable position, touch her back as she curved in toward him.

They slept, awoke, made love, slept again, until early afternoon the next day. That afternoon he worked a long time on his drawing, almost forgetting where he was, except for the comfortable reassuring feeling that he was in a place where he was wanted and liked.

He was able to get a lot of work done, and went to bed that night with a pleased relief that the work was going well. He woke up at two o'clock, by the luminous dial on the table beyond Kate. By this hour, at his home in Upper Dales, Leila's wild party would be in full swing.

Kate stirred, murmured his name sleepily. Gently he drew her close.

"Spence," Kate murmured. "Spence. I love you."

In silence and humble joy, he took the gifts of her body and herself. He did not deserve her; he had messed up his own life, he was ruining her life. But she loved him—in spite of all that he was, all that he was doing to her.

CHAPTER NINE

S PENCE did not go home again till Monday night. He had thought the party would be long over, the house emptied of all traces. He was shocked when he walked in the door.

The smells of liquor, cigarettes and sweat hit his nostrils. The rooms were still blue with smoke. Ashtrays were heaped, over-flowing on the tables. Liquor glasses stood everywhere; some had crashed to the floor, the dregs staining the polished wood and the carpeting.

Dishes of food, glasses, smashed records, bits of clothing were strewn around the downstairs rooms. He went upstairs, stepping over and around more glasses, spilled food, some cigar butts. Cigars? No one in the old gang smoked cigars. Maybe one of the new guys.

He peered into Leila's room. His wife lay sprawled in bed, snoring drunkenly. The room smelled strongly of liquor and sex and smoke. He closed the door quietly. He went to the guest room, ripped the dirty sheets from the bed, threw open the windows to the top. He emptied ashtrays into a wastebasket, added paper tissues, three stockings and a smashed liquor glass. Then he took the wastebasket downstairs and cleaned the other rooms of their accumulated trash.

The house grew cold as he opened all the doors and windows. He put on a heavy sweater and carried out the trash.

It took a couple of hours to air out the place, clean it up, get it looking decent again. Finally he closed the doors and windows and turned up the thermostat until the house was warm.

Some time after eight o'clock he made himself a sandwich and some coffee. He ate in the kitchen, listening to the news on the radio.

He was glad that Leila was still sleeping. When she did awaken, they would probably quarrel. From the looks of it, the party had turned into a two-night orgy. Some of the guests must have stayed till Monday afternoon.

In the quiet house, with the snow falling beyond the windows and clinging to the panes of glass, Spence began to face some truths he had not faced before. Leila loved these parties. She wanted a wild, frantic, riotous existence. She would not change. Any time she acted sweet and loving to Spence she was putting on an act, no more. She wanted her way, and would connive, cheat and lie to get it.

She did not intend to settle down, to try to make their marriage work, to have children, or to be the kind of wife Spence naively had imagined she would become.

Now, mentally placing her beside Kate, he could see Leila clearly. And the picture was ugly. She was not only selfish and devious in her search for pleasure. She lived only for those thrills, for excitement, and did not care who was hurt. If she could have broken up A. E.'s marriage, she would have done so. She was a parasite, living on the fringes of society, beautiful as an orchid, but with not even the usefulness of a flower.

Yet Leila was his wife. Spence groaned, and rubbed his hands wearily over his face. How could he have been such a fool? Just because she was beautiful and warm, and had pretended interest in his work, he had concluded she would make a good wife. Or had he concluded that? Had he used his brain at all? No, thought Spence, he had used less judgment in choosing a wife, had spent less time over the decision, than he would to decide what make of car to buy.

He had married her and he would have to stick it out. Leila would not consent to a divorce, so long as the marriage enabled her to live the gay life she wanted.

At last he turned out the lights and went to bed. But he could not sleep, there in the guest room, thinking of his wife in a drunken stupor and then thinking of Kate as she had been this weekend.

He went back to Kate often from that time on. Leila did not seem to care whether he came home or not. She went her way; he went his.

He spent the next weekend with Kate. Snow had fallen heavily during the week. The deep drifts filled the streets, covered the sidewalks. Traffic in the city was slow, and out toward the suburbs the lines of cars crawled along bumper to bumper, often halted by an accident ahead on the ice-clogged streets.

Kate accepted Spence's explanation without question. "It's a chore to get out to the house. I decided to stay in town this weekend."

She probably knew something was wrong between him and his wife, but she did not ask for confirmation or for details. And for that he was grateful. He did not feel like talking about the situation, a hopeless one, so far as he could tell.

On Saturday he and Kate went for a long walk in the snow, shuffling along in their boots. They had the city practically to themselves. The wind was bitter, a frosty cold gripped the city, the thermometer hovered below zero. But they walked.

"Is this like Alaska?" Spence asked.

"Oh, yes. Only it's so much colder there, sometimes fifty below zero. A deceptive still cold. You can get frostbite without knowing it."

The sun came out, glinting in blinding brilliance off the snowy streets, the snow-covered trees, the white roofs. They found the restaurant where they first had had dinner together. Kate stumbled on the dark steps. Spence caught her.

"Can't see," she explained, laughing breathlessly. "I'm blinded."

"That sun is bright. Here we are." Spence chose a table far enough from the door to be out of the draft. Only a few tables were taken. They ate, lingered over coffee.

Then they walked again in the snow. They peered in shop windows, walked hand-in-hand through a neighborhood park, brushed off a park bench and sat in the sunlight until the cold drove them to walk again.

Kate talked about Alaska, her early days with her family, "when Dad was still with us," the later days when her mother remarried. Spence told her about his life, his work, his friendship with Roy Pritchard.

"You really like him," said Kate. "It must be good to work for him."

"It was," said Spence. "Until recently. Now Cecil and A. E. are taking over, and things are going on that I don't like."

"I'm sorry. I hope it blows over," said Kate sympathetically. She tucked her mittened hand in his arm as they walked along.

"It won't be that easy," said Spence. He said no more about it. They talked of other things, and decided to go dancing that evening.

They went to a restaurant in a hotel near Kate's apartment. The band was good. They danced till after midnight, realized finally that they were the last couple on the floor, and departed.

It felt good to get in bed with Kate, to draw her body close to his tired body, and go to sleep, secure, contented, pleasantly weary.

It was even better to wake in the night, to bring Kate out of sleep with caressing hands, and make love slowly, richly, lazily, and fall asleep still wrapped in her arms. The embrace was less a lust for sex than a desire to share affection in the darkness.

The next weekend Spence stayed with Kate again. Leila seemed quite happy to go to her parties alone, but she told Spence, "Frankly, sweet, you're missing some marvelous girls. There are more new couples. Earl and Leon are having a clear field."

"They are welcome to it," said Spence and packed his suitcase again. Leila watched him narrowly, but made no protest.

Kate suggested rather shyly that there was square-dancing at a dance arena to which she sometimes went.

"Square-dancing?" said Spence, not sure she meant it.

"Yes. Do you like it?"

"I haven't tried it for years. I'm not sure that my bones are still good enough."

They finally went, intending to stay only an hour, and remained till the band quit. The couples were of all ages, ranging from children to a few hardy, white-haired souls who put the younger ones to shame with their skillful and vigorous stepping.

Every now and then during the evening, Spence would get a quick mental image of the party going on at Earl Kennard's house. Flaunted bodies—sensuous music—lustful stares—bold advances—the frantic search for more exotic thrills. The contrast with the gay, fresh enthusiasm of the square-dancers made him feel very odd. There was more than one world in East Burnham. Each person sought and found his own world, where the people were his sort, where he found congenial companionship, the pleasures he liked. If you did not like the company, move on, Spence, he thought. Somewhere the right people can be found.

He smiled at Kate as they "promenaded home." "Tired? Let's sit out the next," he said.

The only refreshments were cold pop, hotdogs and popcorn. The whole evening seemed such a clean, fresh way to spend time that he decided he was sick to death of sophistication. Leila's crowd wasn't his crowd. This was what he liked.

Spence thought he would never forget that evening—the gay happy dancers, the lively music, the quips of the dance callers, and Kate's flushed face and bright eyes and warm hands whenever she met him in the dance.

He spent more and more time with Kate during the next few weeks. They went back to the dance arena for more square-dancing, they went out dancing in other places, went to the movies, walked a lot in the snow and later in the rain. They talked, made love, and slept long hours.

He got in the habit of bringing his work to her apartment and laboring there in the evening and during the weekends. She worked in the kitchen, or cleaned the apartment around him, and he found he could concentrate well on the drawings he was working out.

And when he pushed back his chair, and stretched, and got up to seek Kate, he would always find her willing to come into his arms, ready to be caressed and kissed and held, until they fell across the bed and went on to more radical love-making.

CHAPTER TEN

S PENCE had talked with Bertha Pritchard Foster at great length a number of times since she returned from the Florida trip. They were both convinced that the "vacation" had been for the purpose of setting up price-fixing operations with Pritchard Electric's chief competitors in the field—Locke, Ace and Golden. But Bertha had not been able to force her way into the meetings.

"They don't trust me any more than I trust them," she told Spence sardonically. "And Gilbert has gotten more and more arrogant. I think Cecil and A. E. have made promises to him about managing the company after they force Roy out."

"That means they're planning to force Roy out soon," Spence said grimly.

"I'm afraid so."

Spence stared at the desk top. It was selfish, he thought, but he wondered how long he could hold his job at Pritchard Electric if Roy Pritchard were forced out.

"I asked Gilbert for a divorce," Bertha said suddenly.

Spence jerked his head in surprise. "You did?"

"He refused. He said I had no grounds, that he would fight it. I don't know what to do now. Wait, I suppose. Wait and see what happens."

Things were quiet at the office during the rest of February and the first weeks of March. Then, one Friday morning, Cecil called Spence into his office.

"How's the work going, Spence?" he asked with what seemed forced joviality. "Cigar?" He pushed the cigar box toward Spence.

"No, thanks." For no particular reason, Spence thought of the night he had cleaned the house after Leila's weekend orgy. There had been cigar butts all over the house. "The work is going fine."

"That's fine. I understand you're licking the problem of a compact motor?"

Spence met the shrewd eyes. "We're still working on it. We hope to come up with a good solution." No sense letting Cecil know everything.

"Fine. Fine. Our new products division can be proud of its work. Of course, if we do solve the problem, we still plan to keep the motor under wraps for a year or two."

Spence stared at Cecil's bland face beyond the cloud of cigar smoke. "A year or two? I thought we needed it for the Air Force project. We've been rushing it so we could bid on that."

"Precisely. I understand. But if we use that motor, our bid will have to be high. The cost will be up. And I want the contract."

"Look, Cecil. You don't understand. The Air Force is interested in low bids, sure. But they want this compact-type motor. They'll pay the extra to get it, I'm sure of it. We're way out ahead of competition—"

"It will cost too much to develop it this year. I've ordered the project dropped."

"Dropped? You're crazy! I'll talk to Roy." Spence felt the burning heat of anger rising in him.

"Roy said I should handle this my way. I've convinced him we can make more money by getting the Air Force contract with our old-line motors."

"How do you know you'll get the contract? What if competition under-bids us?"

"That's up to you." Cecil slapped an envelope on the table. "Here's plane transportation to Buffalo, New York. I want you to go to a meeting next Friday. Ace will be there, and Locke and Golden. I told them I want that Air Force contract. It's up to you to convince them it's ours. Then decide on bid prices. We can keep them high, and still be low bidder for the contracts."

"Price-fixing!"

"Precisely. In this day and age, price-fixing is an absolute necessity. The government cuts our throats with taxes, then expects us to bleed to death to live up to its ideas of business competition. All the big companies are doing it. Why shouldn't we?"

"Because it's unethical. It's suicide."

Cecil's smile was cold. "You've lived in a lab all your life. What do you know about business? Well, Roy made you an officer. If you're an officer you'd better begin to act like one. There's a meeting in Buffalo to decide on who gets the Air Force contract and the next two sub-contracts for Royalite Electric Motors. I want you to bring home the Air Force deal. It's time you started earning that high salary Roy says you rate."

Spence felt a cold chill down his spine. He had never expected this. He had sat back and condemned Cecil and A. E. for their business practices. But he had not been personally involved. His work had been an extension of the lab work.

"I'm not involved in getting contracts," he tried to protest. "My job is new products, research and development. I don't know anything about prices—"

"This is a good time to learn," said Cecil. "The cards are down, Spence. You've got to show your hand. Are you going to help us run Pritchard effectively, so we can all make some money for a change? Or are you going to stand in the way of progress? It's as simple as that."

If Spence refused co-operation, he would be fired at once. He wanted to talk to Roy and Bertha first. He temporized. "I'll have to think it over. I'll let you know." He got up to leave.

"Here are the tickets," said Cecil, tossing the envelope at him. Spence caught it, laid it down gently on Cecil's desk.

"Keep them. I may not be using them."

Their stares met. Cecil did not look away. He seemed coldly amused at Spence's inner struggle.

"You don't have a choice, Spence. This is your job. You're an officer of this company. You're to go to Buffalo, meet with the boys, convince them that if they don't let us have low bid we'll spring the new motor and take the bid, anyway."

"You'd use the motor for that?"

"Sure as hell I would."

"Write it out," said Spence. "Write out what I'm to do and say."

Cecil's mouth twisted. "No, Spence. You're a smart boy. You can remember what to say."

Spence called Bertha as soon as he got back to his office. He told her what Cecil had said. "And he won't write down anything on paper. I'll go there cold."

"And if you're caught, the company will deny everything. Sure," said Bertha. "It's a trap, Spence. Don't fall for it. You'll be the scapegoat and be fired for your trouble."

"I'll be fired if I don't go. Damned if I do and damned if I don't. How is Roy?"

"Bad. He mustn't have any excitement, the doctor says. But he's had wind of something and he's upset and fidgety. I don't know whether to talk to him or try to fight it out alone."

"If I could only get Cecil to write it down. Then if anything happens—"

"Dream on, boy. Cecil will never trap himself. Even when we were kids, he could get us all in trouble and keep his own nose clean."

"What do you think I should do?"

She sighed. "I don't know, Spence. For your own good, you ought to quit. But if you go, Dad and I are sunk. I wish you'd stay on a while, anyway."

"I'll see, Bertha. Goodbye."

"Goodbye, Spence."

After he had hung up, he went down to the lab. Ivan Todd was pacing the floor, cursing steadily. No one else was there.

Spence looked around. "Where is everybody?"

"I sent them home. Damn it! Damn it to hell! I was just licking the problem, and Cecil comes in and prances around like a billy goat."

"And calls off the motor project."

"Yeah. Did he ask you about that?" Ivan's usual mask was gone. His eyes were blazing with fury.

"Ask? He told me."

"What the hell's got into him? And why did Roy Pritchard okay it?"

"Something's going on, Ivan. A nice conniving mess of stinky fish. The less you know, the less you'll stink of corruption."

Ivan stared at him. "Hah! So that's it. Intrigue in high places. Plots. Counterplots. Treachery. Treason." Ivan was fast getting back to normal.

"You said it. But keep it under your hat," advised Spence. "And listen. How far did you get with the motor?"

Ivan showed him. "All but the last blueprints for the assembly line. Can you beat that? Just a few lousy drawings and we would be finished."

"Could you take them home, finish them, and lock them up where Cecil and A. E. can't get them?"

"My God, Spence!"

Spence laughed harshly. "I want an ace or two of my own, Ivan."

"Okay. If you say so. I'll gather up all the drawings and take them home. I can finish them nights. Be done in a week or so."

"Then rent a safe deposit box at a bank," said Spence. "Put in all the drawings. The working models—I'll take care of those. If Cecil asks about them, I won't know where they are."

"I will. I'll show him the ones that didn't work." Ivan chuckled unexpectedly. "I knew I was saving them for some reason.

I've got six models that are duds, and the drawings to go with them."

"Good. That's great. And pass the word to the boys not to know anything."

"Right. I'll phone them tonight. You'll see Melvin?"

"Yes. I'll tell him."

"What's going on, Spence?"

"I can't tell you yet."

Ivan looked at him wisely as he started rolling up blueprints. "Don't get your foot in a bear-trap, man. Those things can be mean."

"I'm in one up to my neck."

"If there's anything I can do, any little thing like assassinating Cecil and A. E., just let me know. I have a beautiful do-it-yourself assassination kit."

Spence found himself chuckling as he walked out to his car, carrying two working models of a highly secret motor in a valise. He felt like a cloak-and-dagger character as he put the models in the trunk of the car, then went back for the other two.

It was good to know he was not alone. Bertha would help all she could, and Ivan was no weakling. The Pritchard boys would know they had been in a fight.

He still had not decided whether or not to attend the meeting. Maybe it would not hurt to do so and find out what was going on. Maybe he should let things ride for a while, play along with Cecil and A. E. until he could figure how to out maneuver them.

He locked the trunk after he had the models safely stowed away. Where to put them was the next question.

Kate's. Yes, he would ask Kate to keep them for him. She would. And he had already planed to spend the weekend with her. He hadn't seen her for two weeks, and he was hungry for her.

Leila was having another party at home this weekend. She had not voiced one word of protest when he had announced he would not be around for it. Leila had schemes going also, he figured, but he was too disgusted with her to care. The trouble at the office was enough to worry about for now.

CHAPTER ELEVEN

K ATE SENSED at once that something was amiss when Spence asked her to let him keep a couple of large packages in her apartment.

"Of course, Spence. What are they?"

"Projects. Something secret."

"What's wrong?" she asked quietly. "What has gone wrong?"

"Nothing yet. These are precautions." He tried to smile to ease her concern, but he felt he was grimacing. "Oh, I don't know, Kate. Everything is blowing up in my face."

He went back down to the car in the apartment garage, and brought up the two packages. They were heavy. He made two trips to carry them.

She cleared some space in a storage closet in the kitchen, and they stacked the boxes inside.

She poked a box timidly. "It's nothing that will blow up, is it?"

His grin was not forced this time. "No. There are four motors and they won't run without batteries. Just four hunks of metal parts."

"Oh." She seemed relieved and briskly closed the closet door. "Ivan Todd is always talking so crazily about his experiments, I never know what to think."

"He's a nut, but a nice nut."

"Yes." She smiled, tucked her hand in his arm affectionately. "Can you stay?"

"I intend to."

"Good. Do you want to go dancing, or anything?"

"Whatever you say."

She studied his face with her understanding eyes. "I think we'll stay in. You look beat."

"I feel that way. Not from work, exactly." He sat down on the couch and drew her down with him. He put his hand behind her neck. She bent her head back for his kiss. Their lips met, lingered. He felt the tension draining out of him.

She touched his face with her hand, her eyes half-closed, contented. She was so close, so sympathetic, so undemanding, that on impulse he decided to confide in her.

"Kate, do you know what price-fixing is?"

Her eyes opened wide. "Why, I think I do, Spence. Companies secretly agree on prices that customers must pay, but maintain the appearance of competition. It usually means much higher prices."

"Well—my company is in negotiation with three rival firms to fix prices."

"But that's collusion, isn't it? Punishable under law, and all that."

"Yes. And that's not all of it. See, price-fixing gets around competitive bidding on contract awards. The companies agree not to undercut each other. And they decide in advance which company will get a contract by putting in a bid slightly lower than the other companies."

"I know, dear. I read the papers. There have been some juicy scandals—"

"Next week, I'm supposed to attend a meeting and make sure Pritchard Electric gets the Air Force contracts we've been working for."

All color drained from her cheeks. "Spence, don't do it. Why do they want to get you in trouble?"

He hesitated, startled by her question. "It isn't a matter of getting me in trouble. The company itself will be in trouble. I don't know whether to go or not. If I do, I could find out what's being rigged, maybe stop the operation. As it is, I'm in the dark." He went on to explain his and Bertha's suspicions. "When Cecil Pritchard asked me to go, he told me flatly it was for price-fixing negotiations. But I have no proof. I'm tempted to go, maybe take a tape recorder. I don't know. This cloak-and-dagger stuff goes against my grain."

Kate had been listening in troubled silence. "Oh, Spence, all I know is it's wrong. And I'm afraid the Pritchards are out to get you into a jam. Why did Cecil pick you to go? Why does he suddenly want you to handle sales when you never have before? Why doesn't he go himself? It looks suspicious to me."

He sighed, rubbed his hand over his face wearily. "I don't know, Kate. I don't know what he's up to. I'm no good at this conniving bit. I suppose I should refuse to go. But if I do refuse, I'll be fired—out on my ear after ten years with the company. And they can make it tough for me to get another job in the industry."

"I thought you were friends with their father. Can't he help?"

"Roy Pritchard is a sick man. Bertha fears a shock may kill him. We don't want to go to him except as a last resort."

They talked it out, discussed it from all the angles they could think of. But always Kate came back to her one firm contention.

"It isn't honest, Spence. It's illegal. I think you should refuse to go, no matter what good you think you could accomplish."

"But I might be able to get evidence—"

"If you were caught there, or someone was bugging the session, how you explain your motives to the courts? All they would know is that you participated in the meetings. No, Spence. Don't risk being labeled a crook. You can get another job, I'm sure of it. You're a top man."

"That's easy to say. But I have—" He stopped abruptly. He had been about to say he had a wife to support. "I have financial obligations—a car, a house."

She stroked his hand gently. "I'll sound like a prude, maybe, Spence. But when a car and a house come before a man's honor, he's lost. First things have to come first, let the chips fall where they may." She tried to smile, pressed his hand impulsively against her cheek. "I love you, Spence. I don't want this to blow up in your face. And it would, eventually."

He kissed her. She had said several times that she loved him. He had not been able to answer, because of his sense of duty to Leila. He had not wanted to fall in love with Kate. Life was complicated enough without that. He had not planned on falling in love with her. Meeting her, staying at her apartment, using her as a satisfying mistress, making their affair a matter of sexual expediency—all that was all right, perhaps. But love? No, he had never planned on love.

Yet there it was. He loved Kate, and he could not imagine a happy life without her. What if he never saw her again? What if he had to go back to Leila and the rotten existence in Upper Dales? He flinched, shuddering at thought of returning to orgies, drunken nights, days of sullen hangovers—to angry quarrels, sordid reconciliations.

In bed that night he awoke and saw by the bedside clock it was three in the morning.

He crossed his arms under his head, staring at the darkness. Beside him, Kate slept, her breathing even, unhurried. She was afraid the situation would "blow up in his face." Would it? Or could he manage things so cleverly that Cecil and A. E.'s plans would be defeated?

He sighed impatiently. He was not a clever man. Schemes were for schemers. More than likely, Cecil and A. E. had everything figured. Would it be foolish to try to trick them? Probably so.

But it grated on him to give up so easily, to say meekly, "No, I won't go to the meeting," and be fired and walk out like a lamb, leaving Pritchard Electric to be manipulated by the money-hungry brothers. What would happen to Roy? to Bertha? They would be ousted from any control. The company Roy had founded and of which he had been so proud would soon acquire a blackened reputation.

Surely Pritchard Electric deserved more than that. It was a good company. It had good men working for it. The new motor was a beauty, a really fine contribution to progress. Handled right, it could help boom the company, increase its income, burnish its already shining reputation.

He rolled over in bed, trying to calm his churning mind. He could not stop debating the problem.

Kate touched his chest. "Spence?"

"Yes."

"Can't you sleep?"

"No. Sorry I woke you." He drew her into his arms. She fondled him gently with her warm hands, her fingers stroking over his chest, his arms, over his thighs. He held his breath. She rarely touched him spontaneously, except in the heat of a fierce embrace, when shaken out of her shyness and reticence.

He forced himself to lie still as she caressed his body with her hands, then, growing bolder, she touched his chest with her lips and pressed her cheek against him. Her hands roved timidly, touching, smoothing, exploring with shy determination.

Heat built up in him as she went on. She was a surprise to him. Usually she was passive, waiting for him to move. Now she was a gentle aggressor, her long fingers, her lips, searching, growing bolder.

It was an effort to lie still and not seize her. But he was delighted with her new boldness, and waited to see how far she would go. He smiled in the darkness, let her play until it grew unbearably sweet. Then he drew her over on his body. She was so soft, so warm, so supple, bending her lithe frame to accommodate his.

He rested his head on her breast, heard her heart swiftly beating. Her breathing was coming more rapidly. He played with a pointed nipple, teasing it with his tongue. He put his hand around the breast and moved it roughly, so it was soon swollen. Kate's breathing was quick and deep, her arms tight around him.

"Spence—Spence—I love you."

He wanted to laugh aloud, to cry, to shout, to sing. She wanted him urgently. She loved him. She wanted him, not just for the sexual pleasure, but because she loved him—she didn't want just to use him, to drain him, to punish him, to drag him down with her. She loved him.

He made it slow, drawing it out, holding back, restraining himself, waiting, sliding. He built higher and higher, until her body moved frantically under his, until her hips lunged up at him, until she gripped him with supplicating hands and cried in his ear, "Hurry!"

He helped her—sweet, high, taut, wild, putting pressure on her keenly, sharply. She cried out once more, and fell back, limply, and inside her were quivering convulsions of purest feeling.

The convulsions gripped and released, tightened and loosened on him while he burst, exploded. Blood pounded in his ears. He lay helplessly weak. He had never felt such keen pleasure, such total release. He was blacked-out with the physical and emotional intensity.

He recovered slowly as he felt her soft stirrings beneath him, and realized he had fallen across her body, his head on her breast, legs still tangled. He was heavy, he might hurt her. He forced himself up on his elbows, stared down at her dim face in the dark room.

"Kate," he whispered. "Kate."

She sighed, but could not answer.

He touched her breasts, smoothing the swollen flesh, the hard nipples. He ran his hands down her sides to her waist, possessively. This was his woman, his mate, his companion, his perfect mistress. He crouched up on his knees, ran his fingers over her. She stirred, murmured.

How sweet she was, how willing, how passionate, how gentle, yet stormy. She met him whenever he wanted her. There was no quarreling of their minds or bodies.

"Tell me you love me," he muttered. He kissed her throat, brushed his mouth against her ear, pressed his face in the soft thick hair spread on the pillow. "Tell me."

"Darling, I love you."

He kissed her mouth. "Tell me again."

"I love you," she said obediently. Her arms came up around him, with the limpness of weariness. "Spence. Love."

"Love," he echoed. "Love. Oh, Kate."

"Darling." Her mouth was so soft, so hot, so wet and open and desirable.

"Kate. Sweetheart." His body insisted. She moved. He followed. She yielded.

And in the quietness and joy of the new embrace, he had to say it.

"Kate. I love you."

She seemed to wake, to rouse. She refused at first to comprehend, to believe her ears. "Spence?"

"Oh, yes, yes. I love you. Kate, I love you so much." Her arms tightened, her body received and gave. And it was the love between them that made the embrace so sweet and so long. There was no need to fight and struggle and conquer. The fight was over. Love had won.

CHAPTER TWELVE

O
N MONDAY, it was a rude jolt to walk into the office again. The unsolved problems, the threats, the dangerous decisions, all waited.

Melvin Reed walked in soon after Spence arrived. Melvin's young, open face was troubled. "I didn't understand Ivan on the phone, Spence … Your message about the motor. On Friday and Saturday I kept trying to get you at home but Mrs. Hawk said you weren't there."

"I stayed in town."

"Oh. Well. What did you mean? Is something wrong with my motor? What happened?"

Spence studied the eager boy. No, there was no point in involving Melvin.

"We're not sure yet, Melvin. Ivan and I are going to work it over some more."

"Gee, I'm sorry. I thought I had licked it." He was so disappointed, so obviously distressed, that Spence wanted to spit out the truth. But he knew that Melvin would be better off staying clear of the intrigues. "Gee. I feel terrible about this. I'm not earning my salary."

"Don't talk that way. The motor is a great job. There's just a little work to do on it. So what?"

"Sometimes I think you're only being kind," Melvin burst out. "What have I accomplished since I came here? Nothing. I don't want charity."

"Nobody's offering any," said Spence impatiently. "Your work is good. The motor—"

His phone rang.

"Yes?"

"Spence. Come on over." The receiver banged.

Cecil. Spence scowled. "Damn him, anyway," he growled. He got up. Might as well get this over.

"What's wrong?" Melvin said.

"Cecil wants me to go on a business trip," Spence said evasively. "I don't want to take the time. Besides, it's not my line. Sales—that stuff."

"Oh," said Melvin.

Spence went to Cecil's office. A. E. was there also, lounging in an armchair, his cigar puffing furiously.

"Sit down, Spence," said Cecil. Spence sat down where he could watch the faces of both brothers. Intrigue was foreign to him. He felt uneasy and edgy.

"We thought we ought to brief you on the Buffalo meeting. Who will be there, what you should say."

"Have you written it down?" said Spence brusquely.

"No," said Cecil. "No need for that." He leaned back in his swivel chair and fitted his fingers together in a steeple. "Now, Locke is our most formidable opponent. They're sending Jerry Potts, a tough smooth character."

"He's a sucker for good Scotch," A. E. interrupted. "Be sure to have him up to your room for drinks."

"And there's Ace," Cecil went on.

Spence cut in. "There's no need to go on, Cecil. I'm not making this trip. Sales aren't my baby, and you know it."

"I'm sure you can handle it," said Cecil, his eyes mocking. "Have more confidence in yourself, man."

"I know what I can do," said Spence curtly. "I know my limitations, too. And I draw the line right there."

"You refuse to go?" said A. E. roughly. "You refuse, you bastard? Well, let me tell you, you're not working any more for a soft-headed old man. You're dealing with us, and we don't take any crap—"

"Shut up, A. E.," said Cecil, softly. His fingers tapped, tapped on the desk, the broad, spatulate tips coming down with gentle monotonous precision on the gleaming desk top. "Spence doesn't understand. If he wants to remain an officer of this company, he's got to do the work of an officer. You can't play around in a lab, Spence. You've got to be some real help in management or you don't rate your position. Understand?"

Spence's indecision vanished. The veiled threats showed him where the boys stood. Kate was right. They were out to get him—Spence Hawk—personally. They wanted him in trouble. He had been doing the work of an officer of the company, giving up the lab research he loved in order to do desk jobs, co-ordinate projects, study new ideas, evaluate the progress of the inventions, study the markets. He had worked long hours and had taken his responsibilities seriously. He had been doing the job as Roy had outlined it to him. He had nothing to be ashamed of—and the Pritchard brothers knew it. Cecil was trying to goad him into getting his hands dirty in their new racket, and Spence was not going to dig in the mud to please them.

"You're asking to get fired!" A. E. burst out. He removed the cigar from his mouth to speak more emphatically. "You've had your way with Roy all these years, but let me tell you, you're finished here. If you don't do what we tell you, you're flying out on your can in no time flat."

"Shall I clean out my desk and leave?" Spence challenged in cold fury.

"Now, now, A. E., this is no time for fighting among ourselves," said Cecil blandly. "Let's be reasonable. It's several days before the meeting. There is time to think things over. Spence doesn't want to give up his job, I'm sure. He gets good pay, he has an expensive house and an expensive wife. I'm sure he'll want to reconsider."

Spence burned at the reference to Leila. A. E. grinned mirthlessly.

"Sure," A. E. said. "Sure, Spence. You've got a lot to reconsider. Think it over. Let us know."

"The answer is no," said Spence, getting up to leave. "If I'm fired, call me on the phone. You won't even have to put it in writing."

With that, he walked out. Back at his office, he debated whether to call Roy, finally decided to wait a while longer. He accomplished little work the rest of the day.

He drove home to the expensive house in Upper Dales and to his expensive wife. He longed to be rid of both of them, to be free to work out his life without the pressures of these unwanted responsibilities. But they were there, weights around his neck.

The house was straightened up, for a change. Leila was wearing a becoming blue dress and she did not have a hangover. And she was so sweet and affectionate that he was suspicious at once.

At dinner, she asked, "How's the work going at the office?"

"Fine," he growled.

"I've heard—via the grapevine route—that there's been some trouble."

"Who said so?"

"One of the girls at the office."

Bunk, he thought, and was silent. She persisted.

"What's wrong, Spence? Why won't you tell me?"

"I thought maybe A. E. had already told you," he said coldly.

Her eyes narrowed. "I haven't seen him," she said emphatically.

Spence thought of the cigar butts strewn around the house after several of the parties. "Maybe he phoned you," he said.

"As a matter of fact, he did," said Leila. "He said he was worried about you. You don't seem interested in keeping your job."

"Is that what he said?" Spence wished again he could see inside Leila's mind, open it up and watch the wheels go around, discover what made her tick.

"Yes. He said you seem to feel you can be an official in the company without sharing the responsibilities."

"What else did he say?"

She hesitated, her eyelashes lowered slyly. "He said all they wanted you to do was to represent the company at a meeting in Buffalo. Now it seems silly to me, Spence, that you'd balk at a little thing like that."

"Did he tell you what he wanted me to do in Buffalo?"

"Sure. Talk with some men, arrange about some bids."

"Did he tell you it's illegal, restraint of trade, a violation of the laws?"

She lost her patience. "Don't be a damned fool. I worked at Pritchard for years, and I'm no dumb bunny. Of course, I know the score."

"Then why do you think I should do their dirty work?" Oddly enough, now that she was exploding, his calmness was no longer faked. He was genuinely curious to know Leila's stand in the matter.

"Because you want to keep a damn good job. Because you want to become somebody, not remain a stupid factory hand. I thought when you became one of the managing executives that you would be somebody at last. Instead, you keep fooling around with projects and getting your hands covered with grease. You're just a grease monkey. You want to wallow in the stuff!"

He filled and lit a pipe. The simple act seemed to enrage her.

She jumped up from the table. "Oh, you make me so mad!" she screamed at him. "You could be a big shot—you could earn real money! But no, you've got to turn down this chance of a lifetime. Can't you see? Old Roy is through. You've got to get in good with Cecil and A. E., or you're through, too!"

"You're breaking my heart."

She lifted a dish to throw at him. He stared at her coldly. She finally put the dish down, gripped the back of a chair, and spoke with angry finality, her words hissing.

"Listen, Spence. Listen to me. You disobey A. E.'s orders, and I'm finished! I'll walk out on you. I'll get a divorce!"

He did not dare speak. He did not dare reveal his hope, his hot desire, for her to do exactly that, get a divorce. So Leila had thought of divorce! If he could only, only, get her to go through with it.

"Did you hear me? I'll get a divorce. I'll walk out on you. A word from me, Spence, and A. E. will fire you. And he'll fix it so you'll never get another job! Think it over."

She ran out of the room, slamming the door so hard the dishes rattled on the table.

He sat there smoking his pipe, thinking. Could he count on Leila's divorcing him? No, probably not. She was a shrewd operator. She would never abandon one soft spot without making sure of the next one.

He cleared the table and washed the dishes. Leila did not care how the house looked, but Spence could stand disorder only so long. Later, he went upstairs to bed in the guest room, locking the door. The radio was blaring in Leila's room. She was probably still furious.

He tried to sleep, but his mind was churning. It burned him up to think of Cecil and A. E. getting away with their illegal practices, forcing out Roy, to say nothing of firing him, Spence, for refusing to do their dirty work.

There ought to be something he could do. Something. But there was no proof. Nothing in writing. Nothing definite. Only the motor. The new motor. The Air Force would like that motor, which had been one of Roy's pet projects.

He turned over restlessly. The radio went off in Leila's room. Maybe he could get some sleep now.

Feet padded in the hallway. The doorknob turned gently, then more impatiently.

"Spence! Are you awake?"

What was Leila's stake in this? Was A. E. paying her to encourage Spence to get involved in their shady deals? Had A. E. been attending the parties in Upper Dales?

"Spence?"

He ignored her, folding his arms under his head, staring at the darkness. Was there really a chance that Leila would divorce him, or was that too much to hope for?

"Spence!" She was yelling now, and rattling the knob. "Spence! Damn you, let me in!" Her tone was no longer sweet. It was venomous. He grinned faintly, finding something humorous in the situation.

In his Army days, if anyone had told him he would one day lock his bedroom door against a gorgeous blonde who wanted him, he would have sent the man to a psychiatrist.

He sighed, scarcely noticing when Leila gave up and stamped back to her bedroom.

What hope of having Leila divorce him? What hope of getting the company out of its mess? What hope of going back to Kate with clean hands and saying, "I love you, Kate. Will you marry me?"

Not much hope, unless he could come up with something clever. But cleverness was not his strong point. He could work out motors, invent parts, put things together with his hands, find the balance between economic necessity and laboratory research.

But outwitting two smart and unscrupulous scoundrels— that was something out of his line.

CHAPTER THIRTEEN

S PENCE got up early Tuesday, dressed and left for work. He had breakfast in town. Anything to stay out of Leila's way. Matters were complicated enough without her importunities. He did not want to talk with her about the company. Maybe if she got sufficiently angry at him, she actually would divorce him. At least he could try that tack.

About ten o'clock, Cecil sent for him. Spence curtly sent word that he was too busy to see him. The secretary gasped.

"Do—do you want me to tell him that?"

"Yes. I'm working."

"Yes—yes, sir, Mr. Hawk."

Soon after, the phone rang. It was Cecil.

"So you're too busy to see me, Spence?" said Cecil.

"That's right," said Spence coldly.

"I take it you're too busy to go to Buffalo this week, also?"

"You couldn't be more right," said Spence. He waited for Cecil to tell him he was fired.

Cecil sighed. "I suppose I'll have to go myself," he said. "You're not being very helpful." He hung up.

Spence frowned at the phone. What trick was Cecil conjuring up now? He would never give in meekly. He was up to some devilment, of that much Spence was positive.

There was nothing to do but wait till the outcome hit him over the head. He went back to his drawings. He had been devising another variation of Melvin's motor and he might as well devote the waiting time to working it out.

But Cecil's docility worried him. He brooded about it all day, and he finally reached a decision. He went to Kate's apartment after work.

She was surprised to see him, but glad. She walked into his arms and kissed him, and business flew out of his head for a while.

Later, on the couch, he said, "I've come about the price-fix meeting, Kate."

"You're not going to attend!"

"No. I've refused. I think Cecil Pritchard is going. But I want to fix it so the government knows what's cooking. Are you acquainted with any of the government officials who handle the Air Force contracts?"

She stared at him. "Oh—golly, Spence."

"Are you?"

"Sure. That's my department. My boss could notify them."

"I know where the meeting is to be, the hotel, even the room. It's to be in the suite of Locke's representative."

"Do you want to talk to my boss now?"

He drew a deep breath. Once he started this ball rolling, it could not be stopped. "Yes. I might as well."

Kate telephoned her superior and briefly explained the situation, then introduced Spence. They discussed the matter at length.

"This isn't my field, but I'll call the colonel tonight. I expect he'll want to arrange microphones in the room before the people arrive. You're sure they're going to discuss an Air Force contract?"

"That's the main issue," said Spence.

"I'll get right on it, then. Let's see—Suite 406-8. And your representative is Cecil Pritchard of Pritchard Electric?"

"That's right."

They discussed the arrangements a little longer before hanging up. Spence then wiped his forehead and face. He was sweating, though he felt cold.

"I never did anything like that before," he said ruefully. "I feel like a stool pigeon."

"It's all you can do," said Kate firmly. "It isn't right to let the Air Force be cheated. Why, a difference in cost of fifty cents per motor would mean over four hundred thousand dollars—which the public would pay. That's us. And my tax bills are high enough now."

He tried hard to grin, but he felt sick and uncertain. He felt he was betraying his company—Roy and Bertha, as well as Cecil and A. E.

"Do stop pacing the floor, Spence. It's done now. It was the honest thing."

He sat down on the couch. "I'd better think about getting a new job. I'll be fired as soon as word gets out."

She smoothed his hair back from his forehead. "You're so tired. I wish you could take a few weeks off."

"Go to Alaska," he murmured.

"In March?" She laughed gently. "No, I expect Florida or Hawaii would be better."

He took her hand and kissed it. "I wish we could go somewhere together."

She silently pressed her cheek against his.

The phone rang. She jumped up to answer. "Hello? Oh, yes. Yes. Do you want to talk to him again? Oh, I'll tell him. Thank you. Goodbye."

She replaced the receiver. "My boss. He says it's all set. The colonel is going to have the meeting bugged."

"I sure hope this was the right thing to do," he sighed wearily.

He stayed till ten o'clock, then went home to Upper Dales. Leila was sitting in front of the TV when he walked in. She dashed at him.

"Spence! Where have you been? I was worried sick." She grabbed his coat lapels, her voice rising hysterically. "Why didn't you call? The roads are icy. I thought you were killed—something horrible!"

"I'm all right. I had to stay over in town on business." He tried to remove her hands.

She clung tighter. "Spence, I was so worried. If anything happened to you, I'd just die."

"There is always Leon, and also Earl, to say nothing of A. E.," he reminded her sarcastically.

She pouted beautifully, and he realized the concern and hysteria had been another of her acts. Was she ever honest?

He pulled away from her. "I'm tired. I'm going to bed."

"We've got to talk. You can't keep walking out on me. What did you tell Cecil? Are you going to the meeting?"

"No. I refused to go. They can get their own hands dirty."

"Dirty?" she screamed. "You're a fool! You could have gotten a raise out of this. If you played your cards right, you could even own stock in the company!"

"Who's been telling you fairy stories?" He hung up his overcoat in the hall closet, at the same time watching her face in the mirror on the door.

She smoothed her dress nervously. "Cecil said—that is—I heard that the company is going to expand a lot. When Roy is out, they may make you general manager. And a general manager would get stock. You would have more than just your salary."

Cecil and A. E. had already promised Gilbert Foster the general-managership. Spence wondered how many others had been promised that same plum.

He started for the stairs, but she flung herself in front of him. "No, Spence. Wait. You've got to listen I promised you'd listen to me!"

"Promised who?"

Her eyelashes fluttered. "Cecil," she said.

He knew she meant A. E. "So they want you to talk me into going to Buffalo. Well, no sale. I'm through with playing around. If they fire me, okay. I'll start job-hunting."

"You're a fool!" said Leila, desperately. "Oh, Spence, listen." She caught at his arms, hugged her body enticingly to his.

"Let go."

"No. Listen. I'll be different, I promise. I'll do what you want—give up that crowd. We'll be together again. Just you and me."

"And start a family?"

Her face jerked, smoothed to bland lines. "Sure, Spence. Whatever you say. Only, do as the boys say. They're smart. String along with them, and we'll get everything we want."

He laughed harshly. "Everything you want, Leila—not me. I never wanted to sleep with A. E. Pritchard!" He shoved her out of his path so roughly she was flung against the wall. She cursed him as he marched upstairs, her voice rising hysterically to scream after him.

He went into the guest room, closed and locked the door. Most of his clothes were already in there.

His mouth twisted. Start a family? Like hell Leila would start a family! Once he began doing the dirty work, she and A. E. would blackmail him into handling all the filthy conniving they could dream up. If she did have a baby, it would probably be A. E.'s child. He laughed sourly.

He got into bed, and lay awake again, unable to quiet his restless mind, his aching nerves.

He had burned the bridges. Now let anyone try to cross.

The trouble was, the whole company might go up in smoke, the company he had worked for, served, slaved for, for the past ten years.

What would happen to Roy, to Bertha, to Ivan, to Melvin and all the others?

CHAPTER FOURTEEN

B Y THE FOLLOWING Friday, Spence was as jumpy as a cat
on a burning roof. He jumped every time the phone rang.
There was no one to talk to. Ivan and the others had stayed
home, because there was no work to be done. The lab program
had come to a sudden halt, on orders from Cecil, pending events.
Melvin Reed also was absent. Spence figured he had grown weary
of doing nothing and had taken the day off. He wondered why
Melvin had not said anything to him about it.

He went over to Kate's place and waited in his car in the base-
ment garage until she arrived from work. She smiled when she
saw him but her face was tense with strain.

In the apartment she said, "Have you heard anything yet?"

"No. I don't expect to until Monday, anyway. How soon
would the government act on this?"

"I don't know. The bids are open next week."

"They probably won't move until the bids are in."

"Probably not."

They went out to eat at their favorite restaurant, and afterward danced a couple of hours. Spence had an odd feeling of
finality about this weekend. His life would not be the same after
these few days were over.

What would happen to them all? He would lose his
job. Could he find another one soon? Would Leila walk
out? Should he sell the house, pay off the mortgage, and leave
town?

Alaska. Maybe he could go to Alaska and start over.

Without Kate? What if he never saw Kate again? If Leila decided to cling to the remnants of their marriage as a shabby cloak for her affairs, he would never be free.

The next day, in the afternoon, he was so preoccupied by his worries that it took him a while to realize Kate was unusually silent. She had turned on the record-player. The March rain was drumming against the windows and the sky was so dark he had turned on a lamp to read the paper.

The music was muffled by the noise of the downpour. Kate was sitting in the big armchair, her head resting against the back, her eyes closed as she listened.

He put down the newspaper and saw her lift a hand, rub her forehead.

"Do you have a headache?"

She opened her eyes. "No. I'm all right. Why?"

He shrugged. "You've been so quiet."

"I've been thinking."

"There's nothing we can do now but wait," he said. "No use worrying about it."

"I know. I'm not worried, exactly. You did the right thing. It has to work out right. You did the honest thing. You'll be in the clear, no matter what happens."

He got up and went over to the table for cigarettes. "Do you want to go out tonight? We might find something to go to, a movie or something."

She shook her head. He lit the cigarette, studied her face through the smoke. Something was wrong. She was as transparent as a child.

A wild thought came to him. He walked over to her, touched her face gently. "We haven't been careful. You aren't going to have a baby, are you?"

Scarlet flushed her cheeks. She jerked her head away. "No. My God, no!"

He tipped her face up so he could see her eyes. "Are you sure?"

Her brown eyes met his fully, though her face was as red as her red dress. "I'm sure, Spence. It isn't that."

"I'm disappointed," he said gently. "It would be rough on you—but I've wanted a child for a long time."

He turned away to stare at the rain beating against the windows. It looked cold and chilly outside, bleak and gray and forbidding. Inside it was warm and comfortable, but he did not belong here.

"Spence," she said after a while, "I told you to be honest about the price-fixing, the rigged bids. But we're not being honest with each other."

He stiffened. The record stopped on the player, another one swished on, music began again. "Honest?" he said, carefully.

"Yes. Honest. When we started I knew it was wrong. You're a married man. I should not have encouraged you."

"I didn't require encouragement, as I recall," said Spence. He went down slowly on the couch, looked across the room at her. "The way it was, I kept coming, and you couldn't stop me."

"I wasn't trying to." He knew every curve of Kate's lovely face, every line of her body, the softness of her hair, the sweetness of her movements. It hurt him to see her so tense and sad. "I told you to be honest, but I've been cheating all winter."

"Cheating. You don't know the meaning of the word," he said, thinking of Leila and A. E., Leila and Leon, Leila and Earl, Leila and so many men.

"Yes. You're married. You spend nearly every weekend with me, and some evenings, also. It's as if we were married—but we aren't. It can't just go on and on. You know that."

"Maybe it won't have to. Maybe things will work out soon."

She shook her head. "We should have broken off months ago. I never should have let it get serious."

"It is serious. I love you," he said from across the room.

"I love you too, Spence. It's peculiar. Maybe this would have been all right if we hadn't fallen in love. The morality of the times. Have an affair if you can't manage anything more legal. When you get tired … Oh, Spence, I can't take it any more."

"You're tired of me?" he asked. He felt sick and empty, but he tried to remain calm.

"I'm tired of this set-up. I'm tired of saying goodbye on Monday morning and not knowing when I'll see you again. I'm tired of not being able to call you at the office for fear your secretary will know, will guess—" She choked, put her hands over her face.

He went over to her and pulled her up in his arms. He held her tight while she wept against his chest. He could cope with anger, coldness, fury, deceit, rage, cuckolding—but not with Kate's anguish. He held her, trying to shut out the cold world beyond them. But the cold world remained.

They were not married. They could not be married so long as Leila was Spence's wife. In spite of his and Kate's love for each other, their being together was illegal, immoral, wrong, dishonest. And all the talk in the world could not change the fact.

When she had recovered herself a little, he drew her over to the couch with him. He dried her eyes. She blew her nose vigorously and said, "I'm sorry."

"You're forgiven." He smiled a little, and caressed the back of her neck with his big hand. "What do you want to do, Kate?"

"Now?"

"I mean, about us. Can't we keep on for a while?"

"Drift?"

"Yes."

"I'd rather not, Spence. I mean it. I'm a coward. I can't keep on taking this. It's too tough."

For the first time, Spence looked at the affair from her point of view. She was a sweet, vulnerable woman, loving, generous. She had given and given, against her principles, because she loved him. But what inner conflict it had forced on her! It was tearing her apart. Surely that was not fair to her.

If he were not around, Spence thought, perhaps she would find some other man—a bachelor, a man she could marry. Someone like Ivan Todd. She had dated him quite a long time.

Spence felt a jealous pang at the thought of giving her up to Ivan. No. She belonged to him, not Ivan. Kate loved him, not Ivan. They belonged together; they loved, they needed each other. It would be wrong to turn her over to Ivan Todd.

She leaned back in his arms and pressed her tear-wet cheek against his shirt. Her eyes were closed, the dark lashes glistening. He had hurt her all this time, all the time he had been coming to her for security and warmth and comfort.

Then he knew what he had to do. He had to walk out of her life so he would not go on damaging her. Quickly he attempted to reject the thought, shoving it from him savagely, but it kept coming back. He would have to leave. She would hurt for a little while, but her wounds would heal.

"I guess that's the way it has to be," he finally said aloud.

"How, Spence?"

He brushed his lips against her wet cheek with infinite tenderness. "I've cut you enough. I'd better leave, while you're still in one piece."

Kate's breath caught. He saw the quick movement of the soft mounds of her breast under the red wool.

"But I want this weekend," Spence said suddenly. "I want to stay until Monday." That was selfish, but he had to have this much more, this one last time.

Her arms went around his neck. "Oh, Spence—"

If he fought for it, she would let him come again and again. She could not turn him down. She was not like Leila—deviously plotting to attain her own desires, cunning, dominating. She was too honest to save herself.

"This weekend," he repeated softly. "Then, on Monday—after that, I won't come back. Maybe you can work things out better without me around."

They did not go out that night. They sat on the couch after dinner, and he held her cruelly tight.

"Do you remember that first time?" he said in her ear.

"The snowstorm. And I invited you to stay."

"Why did you?"

"I was lonely. And I liked you, right from the first."

He kissed her cheek and chin and throat. "That very first time, you were so sweet. Your hair hanging down, smelling of soap and perfume."

"I hated myself. I thought what an easy mark I was."

He unfastened the red dress, slipped his hand inside the dress to find a warm full breast. "I couldn't believe my luck. Someone so beautiful and so willing and generous. You are generous, Kate. With your mind, with your body."

"I couldn't forget you. I told you not to come back, but I wanted you so much. You made me feel so complete, so satisfied."

They went to bed, but they wasted no time sleeping. He lay with her, caressing her full soft body, deliberately prolonging their embraces, making them last as long as possible. He explored her with his hands, his lips, as though he had never touched her before.

Their bodies moved under the thick covers, writhed, twisted, met, parted, met again. The rain poured down outside; the sound was cold, insistent, reminding them of the time when each would lie alone, hearing the rain, with no one to turn to in an embrace of forgetfulness.

Her hands came up to clutch his back; her seeking hands, her long searching fingers. Her legs parted once more to allow his body to come between them. The thighs widened, her body moved to a more comfortable position. She opened for him, and he searched, found.

The familiar movements absorbed them, satisfied them. He lay still for her to move her hips in a seeking of pleasure. Then she lay quiet while he played with her. Then in frantic quest for each other, both bodies moved, pressed, clung, crashed together, contested in a soft parody of battle.

But through it all was a strain of sadness, of urgency. These would be the last times. Soon each would lie awake at night, alone, longing, reaching out blindly for the mate no longer to be found.

So they tried with fervent wills and eager bodies to fortify themselves against the time of famine, a famine that might last the rest of their lives.

CHAPTER FIFTEEN

I N SPENCE's life there was an emptiness he had never experienced before, not even during the lonely days of his childhood, the hard-working days of high school and college, the years before his marriage. He missed Kate as he had never missed anyone before, even his parents. He had grown accustomed to her, had grown comfortable in her love, had grown to love and need her as he never dreamed he would need anyone.

He had been restless before, feeling some vague lack, but never the hurt, the void, the bewilderment, that the loss of Kate left in its wake. He had been trapped in a net of his own making. Wanting too much, loving too much, they had hurt each other too much when the time came to tear apart.

The office was a blur to him. He scarcely knew or cared what was going on. One of these days the explosion would roar. He would be fired. He would leave, go some place, try to forget. He waited dully for the blow to fall.

The first week passed with no disturbance or indication of one to come. The second week passed. Spence knew, via the office grapevine, that bids had been sent in on the Air Force contract. From the way Cecil looked, so fat and satisfied, Spence figured things had gone Cecil's way at the Buffalo meeting.

On the third Monday morning following the Buffalo meeting, Melvin Reed dashed into Spence's office. Melvin's face was ghost-white, his hands shaking.

"Spence—I'm going to be arrested!"

"What? What for?" Spence stared at him. He had never seen the young man so upset. "Speeding? An accident?"

"No. No. Price-fixing. They said it was me—my idea. Spence, it wasn't. I swear to God it wasn't my idea."

Spence jumped up and grabbed Melvin's arms. He shoved Melvin into a chair. The boy was trembling so violently that he could scarcely stand.

"How are you involved?"

Melvin chattered incoherently. "They told me—they said I did ... No, no, I didn't—"

"Did you go to Buffalo?"

"Yes. Yes, I went."

"Oh, God," said Spence. "I thought Cecil was going." He felt sick at his stomach. Spence had set the trap and an innocent had fallen in.

"Cecil went. We both went. But it was I who attended the meeting. Cecil stayed in his room. I would go to him. I would ask him what to say, get instructions. Spence, I swear to God I didn't know what was going on!"

"Why didn't you tell me you were going?"

Melvin pressed his shaking hands over his sweaty face. "Cecil—he said you were upset. Couldn't take time to go. I could help, he said. I wanted to help you. I wanted to make up for the motor. Couldn't do anything right, couldn't earn my pay."

Spence felt a chill go right through him. All this was directly his fault. He had wanted to spare Melvin. Instead, he had made the young man feel guilty, had drawn him right to the center of the spiderweb.

"Now—Cecil says the government men bugged the meeting. The bids—rigged—the government's sore, wants to arrest—arrest me! Cecil, A. E. and Gil say the price-fixing was my idea. I swear it wasn't. I swear—"

"You wait here," said Spence. "It wasn't your fault, Melvin. I'll get you out of this if I have to break a few heads." He slammed out of his office, said curtly to one of the wide-eyed secretaries, "Get some black coffee, take it to Melvin Reed in my office. See that he drinks it."

"Yes, sir," she murmured as he went past.

He marched right to Cecil's office and burst in. Cecil and A. E. were talking. Cecil raised his eyebrows.

"I didn't hear you knock."

Spence was not interested in courtesies. He walked up to Cecil's desk and bent over to the bland-faced man.

"You weasel. Getting Melvin Reed mixed up in your rotten schemes."

"I thought it was a master-stroke," said Cecil calmly, his eyes coldly amused. "The poor boy got mixed up, that's for sure. I'm certain by the time the government lawyers get through with him, he'll be convinced he did dream up the price-fixing meeting."

"Melvin isn't going to be your scapegoat," Spence said. "Nothing like that, Pritchard. I'm giving you notice. If you don't clear him, I'm through."

"Too bad. We'll miss you around here," sneered A. E. But Cecil quieted his brother with a wave of the hand.

"Be reasonable, Spence. You're a good man. We would hate to lose you, tough as you are to get along with. Let Reed take the blame. He has been useless around here. He admits that. A few years in jail, a fine. That's all. Why shouldn't he help us out? Why shouldn't he take the rap?"

"Because he did nothing wrong," said Spence, in helpless frustration. How did one explain morality to an immoral man? "Because he is a good worker. He has good ideas."

"His motor doesn't work, the one you wanted us to develop for the Air Force." Cecil watched his face sharply. "We tried it. No good. Why did you try to get us to develop it?"

Spence forced himself to remain expressionless. So Cecil and A. E. did have plans for the motor. It was Roy's motor, Roy's idea for the Air Force project. Were Cecil and A. E. planning to sell it to someone else, someone who might pay a lot more?

"It needs only a few bugs taken out—"

"A few bugs!" scoffed A. E. He leaned forward and tapped his cigar butt in the tray on the desk. "That motor is no damn good at all."

"We're getting away from the point. Melvin," said Cecil. "He's expendable. And he's the one whose voice is on the tapes of the meeting. The Justice Department agents want to make arrests. I've told them the price-fixing was Reed's idea, and we don't approve of it at all."

"You won't get away with that," said Spence. "Melvin told me he had to keep going to you for instructions. That will be in the record. Your name will be on the hotel register."

"No, it won't," Cecil said blandly. "I signed your name. The reservation was in your name, so I used it. If you try to show that Melvin consulted anybody"—he pointed his cigar at Spence—"you'll only damn yourself. You see, boy? All the angles. Why fight us? You're licked before you start."

Spence stared at him. Then he leaned across the desk and hit Cecil so hard it knocked him out of his chair. The man went sprawling foolishly into a corner. A. E. jumped up and grappled with Spence. Spence knocked him down also, so hard he bounced. Soft, both of them. Soft, as spiders in their webs.

He waited angrily for them to get up so he could knock them down again. They glared at him from the floor, neither one daring to get to his feet.

"I warn you," he told them. "If you let Reed be the scapegoat, if you let him be arrested and take the rap, I'll walk out. And I'll devote plenty of time to making you pay for this. You may be clever but you won't get away with it."

Spence walked down the hall to his office. He sent Melvin home with Ivan Todd, then went out to a hotel to call Bertha. He briefed her on what had happened.

"Oh, my God, Spence. That's horrible. Poor Melvin."

"We've got to tell Roy now. This thing has gone too far. I should have told him long before this."

"Yes." She hesitated. "Father knows something is going wrong. I'll tell him. You come on over, Spence. I want to talk to you, too. We'll have to figure out something."

Bertha had been staying at the Pritchard home for the past couple of months. Spence figured she was not living with Gilbert any more, but he had heard nothing further about a divorce.

Bertha herself let him in. She was thinner than ever, looking haggard in a black crepe dress, a cigarette trembling in her thin fingers. "I told Dad, Spence."

"How did he take it?"

Bertha took Spence's overcoat and hung it on a hall rack. "Quietly," she said. "But he's started that shaking again. I'm scared. I called the doctor. He should be here soon."

They went to Roy Pritchard's study. The old man was seated in a plump leather armchair, his head against the back rest. His face was waxy white except for the brown spots of age that marked his cheeks. His hand was cold when Spence held it briefly in greeting.

"Spence. It's been a long time. You don't come to see me as often as you used to."

"I'm sorry, Roy. It's been a rough winter."

The old man nodded. "I guessed something was wrong, but nobody would tell me anything. I kept hoping you would come and give me the score. You always used to tell me the truth, even when it was bad news." He smiled briefly, his pale lips moving tiredly.

"It's damn bad news this time, Roy. Bertha told you about the price-fixing?"

"Yes. I never would have condoned it. Never." He tried to clench his fist and hit it on the arm of the chair. "Those boys. Cecil always wanted to make money the easy way. He's too lazy.

And A. E.—always chasing women. Doesn't care if the business goes to hell."

"Please, Dad, don't get yourself excited," Bertha begged.

"What about my motor, Spence? Is that bad, too?"

"No, Roy. It's a beaut."

"What?" Bertha stared. "Gil told me last week it was a failure."

Spence grinned. "I guess you'll think I've plumb lost my honesty. But I hid the new motors, the real ones. What Cecil saw were the failures."

"God damn," Roy cackled, some color staining his cheeks. "You sure fooled 'em! Do those motors really work?"

"They really do. I've hid them, and Ivan Todd put the blueprints in a safe-deposit box at a bank."

Bertha laughed delightedly. "You really did it! Oh, I'm so glad."

Don't tell anyone," Spence warned. "We're saving the motor for an ace, in case we need a better bargaining position. Besides, I figure it's Roy's motor, not Cecil's."

Roy looked surprised. "Yes, it's my idea. But the company—I always thought it was for the company—" His voice trailed off. He leaned back wearily.

"We've got to figure out something," Bertha said. "It makes me furious to think of Cecil and A. E. getting away with murder. Let's call a special stockholders 'meeting."

Roy disagreed. "I haven't got the strength for a fight of that kind. Two against two. They have half the stock, we have half. Stalemate. No, we'll have to figure out something else."

"One thing is sure," Spencer said grimly. "Melvin Reed must not take the rap. If anyone was ever an innocent bystander, he is. And he solved the motor problem, you know, Roy."

A spark of interest flared in Roy's eyes. "He did? He designed the new one?"

"Yes. Came up with several new angles, kept working them out, had a real brainstorm and got rid of the big bug. And here we've been trying to figure out that motor for years! Melvin's a good man, Roy. I would hate to see him kicked around."

"Yeah. Yeah. Well, we'll work it out some way."

A few minutes later the doctor was shown into the room by a maid. Bertha greeted him with relief.

"I just wanted you to make sure dad's all right. He's had a shock."

Spence felt he was getting nowhere. "I'd better go," he said.

"Goodbye, boy. Don't be so long coming again."

Bertha showed Spence to the door. "Now, don't worry. Dad's body is wearing out but his mind isn't. He'll think of something."

"Sure he will." Spence was not too convinced but he tried to hide that. "Thanks a lot, Bertha. We'll keep fighting all the time."

"Right." She smiled and her eyes sparkled. She could be an attractive woman when she was not giving way to bitterness and resignation. "I'll call you soon. And keep in touch with me. We'll pool our information."

Spence went out to his car. Rain was falling again, a cold determined March rain that soaked the ground and pounded the trees and the car. He switched on the lights to drive through the blinding downpour.

The whole situation seemed so hopeless. Bertha talked of fighting, but Cecil and A. E. still held most of the cards. Bertha had not mentioned Gilbert, her husband. Did he influence her any more? If he did, since he was working hand in hand with the Pritchard brothers, Bertha would not be much help.

And Roy. He was old and feeble. The shock this afternoon might have been too much for him. What could he do? What could he dream up? In his prime he had been a clever, original thinker, an inventor, a good businessman. But now ...

Spence figured he might have to fight the rest of the way alone.

CHAPTER SIXTEEN

L EILA was waiting at the door when Spence walked in. There was no meal ready. She started in on him as soon as he shut the door on the pouring rain.

"You fool. You big, dim-witted bastard."

He sighed. He was in for a long session tonight. "And how are you, Leila?" he asked mockingly. "Did you have a nice long talk with A. E. today?"

"Yes, I did," she blazed back. "I went to the office and talked to him, and to Cecil, too. You crazy, stupid fool! Hitting them—knocking down the people you work for! Is that your idea of getting ahead in the world? You're so stupid. All you can do is use your fists."

"Yeah," he said. "I'm not smart like Cecil and A. E. I don't believe in being a perjurer or a crook." He went out to the kitchen to make himself a sandwich.

Leila followed him, high heels clattering on the tiles. A radio was on upstairs, full blast. Why was this house always so noisy?

"How do you expect to support me without a job?" she demanded.

"Oh, am I fired? The boys didn't tell me. Is this the official word?"

He eyed her sardonically as he got out the coffeepot. He enjoyed baiting Leila, making her trap herself, now that he knew what she was and where she stood.

"You don't expect to stay on at Pritchard, do you? After slugging Cecil and A. E.? What kind of a privileged character do you think you are? Don't tell me that you expect any help from old Roy."

He shrugged. No, he could not expect much from Roy. About all he could do was make a clean breast of everything to the government men and try to get Melvin off the hook. Then he would pull up stakes and move on—somewhere, anywhere.

"Well, I warned you. Don't say I didn't warn you!" She stamped her pretty foot.

"You warned me. Want a sandwich?"

"No. You seem to think this is funny. It isn't. And I'm through with you! I told you I'd be through if you didn't do what the boys wanted."

"I seem to remember some vague threats," he said wearily. "Don't we have any peanut butter?"

"Vague threats? I'll show you how vague they are. I'm going to get a divorce."

"Care to bet on it?" he said flippantly. "Oh, here it is," he said, finding the jar of peanut butter behind the cans of fruit.

She cursed him. "You bastard! I'm sick to death of you. Always spoiling my fun, thinking it's funny to spoil everything I want. Always being sarcastic. You're a cold fish. I don't know why I ever married you."

"I've been wondering myself. You love money so much, and I don't have any."

Leila's laugh was a short bark. "You aren't kidding. I'll be more careful the next time." She perched on a kitchen chair, her eyes narrowed, her face coldly calculating. "Okay, I'll get a divorce. Let me have the house and the furniture, and we'll call it quits."

He was tempted, but decided to bargain. "They aren't paid for. And you forget—I'm out of a job. You want to take over the payments?"

She scowled, biting her underlip. "Hell, no."

"I could put it up for sale. If I clear enough to pay off the mortgage on the house and the furniture, that's all I can expect. More likely I'll have to dig up some more to pay off the loan."

"Will you agree to give me half your earnings as alimony?"

"Twenty-five percent," said Spence, still bargaining. "It won't matter anyway, if I don't have a job."

"Hell," she said. "How much do you have in the bank?"

He took out his checkbook. "One hundred forty-three dollars and sixty-two cents."

"My God, Spence, I can't get a divorce on that."

"Maybe A. E. would lend you the money," he suggested ironically.

Her calculating look appeared again. He wondered if A. E. had already given her some money.

"I'll see. Anyway, I'm going south right away. I know where I can get a divorce there in a couple of days."

So she had been checking. He was beginning to be hopeful. That evening she started packing her suitcases.

"I may sell the house while you're gone," he told her, standing at her bedroom door. "Why don't you pack everything?"

"What would I do with the stuff?" she said, exasperated. "I can't take it along."

"Maybe one of your friends—Amy, or someone—would keep it."

She came over to him, leaned against him. "Oh, Spence, I don't really want to leave you. Why don't you call Cecil, tell him you're sorry? We could patch things up."

He was not moved. He felt no desire for the luscious full body pressed so enticingly against his. "No. I'm going to get fired. Then I'll pull up stakes, maybe go to Alaska and look for work there."

"Alaska?" screamed Leila. "Where do you get such crazy ideas? That barbaric place—"

"It's good, big, clean country," said Spence. "Lots of snow and ice. There's a need for men who can work with machines."

She went back to her packing...

She left a couple of days later. After Spence had taken her to the airport and had seen her off, he stopped at a real estate office.

"I want to sell the house and furniture, everything. And I want to sell fast. If anyone wants the house, bring the price down far enough to suit him. Just get rid of it."

"All right, Mr. Hawk. But it's a beautiful home—and such a lovely suburban area, such cultured people—"

"You can have them all," said Spence, and gave him a hotel address in town. "I'll be moved out by tomorrow noon. I'll drop off all the keys then. I never want to see that house again."

"What about Mrs. Hawk?" the agent asked, in distress.

"She's getting a divorce."

"Oh. Oh, I see. I'm terribly sorry. I'm so sorry, Mr. Hawk." The agent's face turned red.

"Don't be. I'm not." He left as the agent, speechless, stared after him.

Spence spent the day making arrangements and packing the few possessions he wanted to keep. He went to sleep on the uncovered mattress in the guest room. The rooms were stripped of linens, cushions, pillows, curtains, lamps, the radios, the TV set. But Leila had not wanted the furniture. She was "sick of the same old things." The agent had said he would sell the furnishings with the house.

Spence felt light-hearted in spite of the grave situation at the office. Leila had left. She had promised to call when the divorce was granted. She seemed as anxious to end this marriage as he was. And she had plenty of money. He had seen a large bankroll in her pocketbook when she had paid for her plane ticket. A. E. must have come through.

Spence longed to call Kate, but he wanted to wait till he could go to her and tell her the divorce was final and definite.

He slept dreamlessly that night—his last night in a house that he had bought with such high hopes. He had always planned to turn one bedroom into a nursery. Instead of the sound of a child's voice echoing through the house, there had been the crash of liquor glasses, the throbbing of bongo drums, the rhythms of sensuous music, the raucous laughter that signaled debauchery.

That was over for him. Finished.

As for the mess at the office, something would work out. Somehow he would set things straight, get Melvin out of that jam.

Then he would leave, move on—with Kate. They could start again some other place, where he was not known, where the Pritchard boys could not reach. Alaska?

CHAPTER SEVENTEEN

LEILA did not telephone. Spence felt more and more uneasy as the third, fourth, fifth day passed. Finally on Tuesday morning, she phoned the office.

"Hello, darling," said the familiar, cooing voice.

Spence felt a cold chill go down his spine. "Leila? Where are you?"

"Back in town, darling. At the Royal Hotel, room nine twenty-six, in case you want to come up."

"Didn't you—get the divorce?" he managed to choke out.

"Of course, darling! That's why I called you. I have all the papers. You talked to my lawyer, didn't you? He said he had your signature."

A great breath of relief swept through him. He sank back in his swivel chair. "Yes. Yes, I talked to him. So it's final now?"

"In effect, darling," Leila caroled gaily. "It will take a few days for the actual decree to come through. I'll bring the papers to your office this afternoon."

"You don't need to. I'll get them from your lawyer," he said hastily.

"It's no trouble, sweet. I'm coming up, anyway. I want to talk to A. E."

Well, it was no longer any business of his. "Whatever you say, Leila."

"Did you sell the house?"

"Yes. It wasn't quite enough to pay off the mortgage, but I guess I can pay off the rest during the next year or so. If I can find another job," he added grimly.

"Poor sweet. You never did learn how to manage money, did you?" she cooed. "Well, I'll see you this afternoon."

She hung up. Spence frowned, but he felt relieved. He had been on edge for fear Leila would change her mind. He telephoned her lawyer for confirmation. The lawyer confirmed that the matter was all settled.

Spence's hands were trembling when he hung up. He wanted to call Kate, to rush out to the Field to see her, and tell her. But tonight would be soon enough.

Wait. A job. He had better hold off until he was sure that he was capable of supporting a wife.

Bertha rushed into the office. "Spence—Melvin's been arrested. I just heard."

That news blotted all else from his brain. He roared off to Cecil's office and stormed in. Cecil and A. E. were sitting there licking their lips.

Spence roared, "You dirty, conniving bastards! I told you what I'd do if you didn't let Melvin off the hook—"

Bertha, following, caught his arm as he moved in to trounce them. "No, wait. Wait, Spence." She pulled him back. "My father is coming. We'll talk. Wait—"

"Wait, hell! I've been wanting to have a showdown with these guys—"

"You're fired," said Cecil hastily, putting two heavy chairs between them. "You're fired, right now. If you lay a hand on me, I'll call the police."

At that moment, a secretary wheeled Roy Pritchard into the office. The sight of Roy in a wheelchair made Spence blink.

"What happened? Roy! Why...?"

Bertha said, "Take it easy. The wheelchair was my idea. The doctor said it would make it easier for him to come to the office."

"Suppose we sit down and talk things over," said Roy, with the old tone of authority in his voice that made them numbly obey him. "I've had several ideas about this affair, Spence. I talked to Cecil and A. E. a couple of days ago, you know."

"You're not going back on your word, are you?" A. E. said angrily.

"Do I ever?" Roy looked at his stepson with cold distaste. "Gilbert has already left to get a divorce from Bertha. When he returns, Bertha and I will turn over certain Pritchard Company stocks to him. The rest we will sell to you."

"No!" said Spence. "No, you can't give up like that!"

"Hear me out," said Roy. "Bertha has been wanting a divorce for a long time. Gilbert wants stock in the company. And the way Cecil and A. E. are running things, neither Bertha nor I care to be associated here."

Spence was stunned. This was the last thing he had expected Roy to do—to run out, to give up without a fight. He sat silent as the boys wangled with their stepfather.

"I want your assurance that Melvin Reed will be cleared," said Roy. "Otherwise, I don't sell."

"You've already agreed to sell. Besides, if you stay, then we can outvote you—Gil and A. E. and me. You haven't a chance."

"Gilbert doesn't have the stock yet," said Bertha.

"Want me to call him and tell him so?" Cecil sneered. "He can always call off the proceedings."

Bertha shrank back in her chair, looked at her father helplessly. The argument could not be settled. Roy was getting tired. Spence finally broke in.

"We're not getting anywhere. Let's go back to my office."

He wheeled Roy out, Bertha following. At his own office, Spence asked his secretary to order some hot lunches sent up, then helped Roy lie down on the couch. Bertha covered him with a blanket.

"We're not licked yet," Roy said in a feeble voice.

"Of course not, Dad," said Bertha, patting his hand.

"Tell—tell Spence what we're planning," Roy urged his daughter.

"Oh, hell, yes. In all the excitement, I forgot." She smiled.

"Good news? I could stand some," said Spence wearily. He was worried sick about Melvin Reed. That poor kid.

"Spence—Dad and I talked a long time, explored every angle. Finally we agreed on what we had to do. Pull out of this company, since we can't outvote Cecil and A. E. Then form a new company—and run it the way we want to."

"A new company?"

Roy was beaming. "Yes," he said, with his old enthusiasm. "Start over again. I'm getting old, but Bertha's keen to try it. She's going to put her money in it, too, plus what Cecil and A. E. give us for the sale of our holdings in this company, understand?"

"And we want you!" Bertha turned to Spence. "We were going to steal you away"—she laughed excitedly—"but Cecil saved us the trouble by firing you!"

"You want me, after the way I messed up—"

"We can't do it without you," said Roy. "We need an engineer to head this. Bertha can handle the personnel and get someone for sales. But what will we sell if we don't have you to develop new products and shape the line?"

Spence sank down in his chair. His knees felt flabby and useless. "My God—I—I don't know how to thank—"

"The way we figure," Bertha broke in, "You should own stock in the new company, as an incentive. You'll be general manager, with voting stock. We won't be short of money, by any means. We feel we can start you at five thousand a year higher than your present salary. Will you do it?"

Spence opened his mouth but no words would come. Bertha laughed at him teasingly. Roy was grinning from ear to ear. Spence's secretary came in with the office boy and hot lunches. The three owners of a new enterprise babbled excitedly while they ate. Ideas—plans—an office—

"We'll work from home at first," Bertha said. "We'll take our time to find a place or maybe build a plant with a lab and offices."

"Take it easy!" Spence groaned. "You're spending money like water."

"I hope we can steal away Ivan Todd, too," said Bertha cheerfully. "He's utterly mad, but he's a wonderful worker."

"The motor," said Spence. "We'll have the new motor!"

"That helped give us the idea," said Roy. "With that motor we can grab several new contracts. The problem will be manufacturing."

"What's that noise out there?" said Bertha. Someone was screaming in the hall. Bertha opened the door and peered out.

"I'll show you! I'll show you bastards!" It was Leila, screaming back over her shoulder at A. E. and Cecil as she came toward Spence's door.

"Spence!" she cried.

He sighed. "Hello, Leila."

She came in and slammed the door.

"What's the trouble, my dear?" said old Roy Pritchard mildly.

"Those—those damn bastards. They promised me stock. Now they've reneged. I'll show them."

"Stock for what? What were you supposed to do?" asked Spence sharply.

She was too angry to be discreet. "I was to try and persuade you to do their dirty work. I did try—I did! Now the filthy cheats won't pay up."

Spence gazed at her in silence. She fumbled some papers out of her handbag and threw them on the table. "Here are your copies of the divorce papers, Spence. Damn it, anyway. I had it all figured out." She was like a child who had not won the prize at a party game.

"You got a divorce?" said Roy, lifting his head.

"Yes. Now that Spence is fired, he can't support me." She shrugged. "I'll have to find myself a job. Oh, hell."

"You should have stuck with Spence," said Bertha.

"Why?"

Bertha hesitated, looking uneasily at Spence.

"We're starting a new company," Spence said boldly. "Bertha and Roy want me to be general manager, with stock, and at a higher salary."

"Pritchard and Hawk," said Roy, unexpectedly. "I like that. Let's call it Pritchard and Hawk."

Leila stared, wide-eyed. "You mean—you mean—Oh!" She flung herself at Spence, embracing both him and opportunity with boundless enthusiasm.

"There's just one problem," said Spence, smart at last. He felt Leila owed him, or Melvin, something.

"What, darling?" cooed Leila, with wide adoring blue eyes.

"Melvin Reed has been arrested. If we could get someone's testimony that Cecil or A. E. planned that—"

"I could tell you," Leila said promptly. "A. E. called me—oh, lots of times—and he wrote me, too. I have the letters. A. E. told me when you refused to go to that meeting, Spence, that he talked Melvin into going. I have that in a letter. And Cecil registered at the hotel under your name. I know that."

Spence immediately called Roy's lawyer. An hour later he was in Spence's office with a secretary and a tape recorder. Without a tremble, a quiver or a regret, Leila told all she knew about the machinations of Cecil and A. E. Bertha and Roy and Spence sat and listened to her confession.

"So I promised to try to get Spence to stay on and do what they said. A. E. suggested I should threaten to divorce Spence. That would bring him around, A. E. said. So I tried that. But Spence got all the more angry at me, and told me to go ahead and get a divorce. So I did," Leila finished.

The secretary shut off the recorder.

Leila said, "There. That will teach those characters to laugh at me!" She was still furious with them.

Bertha and Roy left with the lawyer, promising to take care of Melvin's release as quickly as possible. Leila, who had been carrying A. E.'s letters in one of her suitcases, had already turned them over to the lawyer. Spence wondered amusedly what Cecil and A. E. had been doing all afternoon while Leila had been spilling the beans. They had probably been sitting in their offices, counting their money and weaving more spider-webs.

Spence could predict the future of Pritchard Electric. Cecil, A. E., and Gilbert were not good engineers, inventors, researchers. They could stumble along for a while with their present products. But the health of an electrical company depends much less on clever financial manipulations than on new ideas, new products. If Ivan Todd and Melvin Reed and Spence all walked out and took the lab boys along, there would be no one left to do the vital work.

Everyone, by now, had left the office save Leila. She closed the doors, returned to Spence. She leaned against him, putting her arms around him.

"Oh, Spence, I've been so wrong," she murmured. "Please forgive me for all the terrible things I said."

He stood still. He felt nothing for her any more. She was finished business for him, an experiment that had failed.

"Nothing to forgive, Leila. I appreciate your testifying for Melvin."

"I was glad to. The poor boy. I hope he gets off soon."

"He will now."

Her arms tightened. "Spence, I'm sorry already about the divorce. Why don't we go up to my hotel room and talk about it?" Her voice was husky, suggestive.

Gently he freed himself from her arms. "No, Leila. We're through. We had better go our separate ways. We don't like the same things. You know that."

She frowned, pouted. "Oh, Spence, we could start over again."

"No," he said definitely. "If I marry again, I want to settle down and have a family. No more mad parties, nothing of that kind. You wouldn't like the tame life I'm planning."

Her mouth twisted. "No, I guess I wouldn't," she said frankly. "Do you mean it, Spence? No more parties, no more fun?"

"Not that kind of fun, Leila."

She shook her head. "I guess we are finished then. Where will I go?"

"Why not New York?" he suggested. "Or California? They like wild parties, I hear."

She brightened. "That's an idea. California. I could get a job with a movie production outfit—work for a producer."

"Sure you could. And don't forget that until you find somebody else to marry, as we agreed, you get a quarter of my income. That won't be hay, now."

She kissed him goodbye. "But come up and see me before I go, Spence. You're a swell lover when you want to be. We could have a great time."

"Don't expect me," he said. "I have work to do."

CHAPTER EIGHTEEN

Roy Pritchard's lawyer was able to convince the government that Melvin Reed was innocent of any involvement in an attempt to fix prices and rig bidding. Charges against him were dropped, new charges filed against Cecil Pritchard. It would probably take a long, involved legal battle to prove conspiracy to defraud the government, but Spence had some hope that Cecil would at least be caught in one of his own webs.

Spence was through with the Pritchard boys. During the week following Melvin's arrest, he and Bertha worked with Roy on the business of setting up a new firm, planning the new projects, and hiring the new employees. Ivan Todd was the very first one—he had managed to get himself fired from the old firm in record time. He came over to Roy Pritchard's home, beaming, and spouting his mad-scientist talk.

"I had a marvelous idea. I'll hook up Cecil's brain to a sound-wave generator. Then we'll beam these waves abroad. See, the sounds will be so crooked they'll drive all our enemies insane."

"There's only one thing wrong with that idea," scoffed Bertha.

"Wrong with it? What could possibly be wrong with any of my masterful ideas?" said Ivan huffily.

"Cecil is so lazy the machine would work only a few minutes a day."

Even Roy laughed. Ivan eyed Bertha with awed amazement. "You are a genius. Together we can make marvelous inventions."

Bertha blushed. Spence watched the pair with suddenly aroused interest. Ivan was a bachelor, a really wonderful guy who had never found the right woman. Bertha was a woman who had been deeply hurt by the wrong man… But that was none of his business, Spence decided.

Leila had soon departed for California, after trying in vain to entice him to her hotel room. Evidently she had decided he was no fun any more and she might as well start over again elsewhere.

Spence had been busy day and night with getting Melvin cleared, starting the company, lining up the first projects—to include the new motor—and keeping an anxious eye on Roy so that he would not overtax his strength.

Melvin was happy and dazed when he learned the truth about the motor, and a little incredulous. "I won't believe it till I see the thing work."

"I'll bring them here to Roy's on Monday," Spence promised. "I'm going to take Sunday off. We've worked enough this week." It was late Saturday afternoon and he thought everyone looked bushed, especially Roy.

The meeting broke up soon after that. Spence drove back into town and headed for Kate's apartment. Their meeting was long past due. He had a moment's worry for fear she might be out with someone else. But at the same time he felt serenely confident that she still loved him. He was positive that the love between them had been too deep to have vanished so soon.

He drove down the ramp into the parking garage under the apartment building. He parked the car at the usual place.

He walked over to the telephone and rang Kate's apartment. "Kate?"

"Hello—not you, Spence!"

"Yes. May I come up?"

A silence. Then she said, "If you think it's wise."

She sounded subdued and tired. He took the elevator, and she was standing in the doorway of her apartment when he arrived.

Beyond her, he saw a green vase of jonquils and tall spikes of pussywillows that gave the place a look of spring, and then he suddenly remembered it was April.

"Did you come for the motors?" she asked.

"Oh, yes. I want them."

She waited for him to say something more, her brown eyes thoughtful.

"I wanted to ask you to marry me," said Spence.

Her eyes widened. "What?"

"Leila got a divorce. I'm free. The company blew up. Roy and Bertha and I have formed a new company. Will you marry me?"

"Oh—Spence! Are you crazy—or just drunk?" She was completely bewildered, incredulous.

He started to laugh. He grabbed her arms, pulled her close. "Oh, Kate, say you'll marry me—or I really will go crazy."

She put her arms around his neck, looking up wonderingly at his face. "Just tell me once more—you are free? She did get a divorce?"

"She did."

"Oh, Spence. Oh, I can't believe—" She started to cry. He stopped that with a long, rough kiss.

When they were both more calm, she wanted to hear all about everything, including Melvin's arrest, what everyone had said, what old Roy had done, how it had all ended.

"Mr. Pritchard must be a wonderful person," she decided.

"Roy? He's tops. And to think I believed he was through! I was as bad as Cecil and A. E., underrating him. I want you to meet him soon."

"I'd love to. And what did Ivan Todd do?"

"He threw in with us. And Melvin, of course. Melvin still can't believe his motor is okay. I want to take our prototypes over to Roy's on Monday and hook them up for the kid."

"Poor Melvin. He got the worst deal."

"He sure did. We want to make that up to him." But Spence was tired of talking of other people. "Did you miss me, Kate?" he demanded.

"Miss you? Oh, Spence."

"Tell me you love me."

She told him, several times.

"We could get married next week," he said, "Gosh. You haven't said you'd marry me."

She laughed at him tenderly. "Do you have any doubts?"

"I don't know where we'll live. I sold the house. I got to hate that place."

"It was in the suburbs, wasn't it? Way out in Upper Dales? I'd rather live in the city. I think they have better schools," she said seriously.

He grinned. "Schools. What for?"

She blushed. "I thought you said you wanted children."

"I sure do. How soon do you suppose we'll have a baby?"

"Spence! Really!" She was blushing prettily.

It was not even six o'clock in the evening, but they decided it was quite time to go to bed.

THE END